The Journey

The Journey

An Eleutherian Experience

SHARON FARQUHARSON

authorHOUSE®

AuthorHouse™
1663 Liberty Drive
Bloomington, IN 47403
www.authorhouse.com
Phone: 1-800-839-8640

Published by AuthorHouse   01/04/2013

ISBN: 978-1-4817-8093-3 (sc)
ISBN: 978-1-4817-8092-6 (hc)
ISBN: 978-1-4817-8094-0 (e)

Dedication

I dedicate this book to the communities of Eleuthera, Spanish Wells and in particular Harbour Island, Bahamas.

Acknowledgements

The support of persons like Dr Chaswell Hanna, Adjunct Lecturer at the College of the Bahamas; Mrs. Paulet Wilsher, Senior Lecturer, Early Years Professional and Researcher in the UK; Ms. Sasha Dixon, Third Secretary at the UN and Mrs. Lenora Brown, Senior Officer at the Ministry of Education, Science and Technology, Nassau Bahamas. They encouraged and assisted me in bringing this book to fruition. Special thanks to my husband Paul Farquharson, QPM for his patience and inspiration.

About the Author

Sharon Farquharson holds a Bachelor of Science Degree in Social Work from the University of the West Indies, Jamaica, a Diploma in Public Administration from The College of The Bahamas, A diploma in Life Coaching from the Home Learning College, United Kingdom and a Masters Degree in Human Services, Nova University, Fort Lauderdale.

A veteran Social Worker/Administrator, she served in the Departments of Social Services and Rehabilitative Welfare Services for 38 years. For 9 years she was an adjunct Lecturer at Sojourner Douglass College, Nassau Bahamas.

In her role as social worker and adjunct lecturer she touched the lives of many families and adult students. As Director of Rehabilitative Welfare Services she inspired her staff to strive to be the best public officer that they could be and to perform their duties at a high standard.

Mrs. Farquharson is a devout Christian and served as Sunday School Superintendent for 5 years at St. Gregory's Anglican Church, Nassau Bahamas, Lay Director of the Bahamas Anglican

Cursillo Movement and a member of St. Gregory's Church Prayer Group.

She is married to Paul Farquharson QPM, former Commissioner of Police in The Bahamas and recently retired High Commissioner for the Bahamas to the United Kingdom. They have 4 children and 8 grand children.

Foreword

As High Commissioner to London for the country of Antigua and Barbuda, I am very pleased to have been invited to write the foreword for 'The Journey: An Eleuthera Experience' written by Sharon L. Farquharson.

The publication is intended to share with the wider community in The Bahamas but most of all the children and the tourist that visit The Bahamas.

The story reflects on the islands of Eleuthera, Harbour Island and Spanish Wells focusing largely on each island's historical sites. Additionally, mention is made of the political, social and economic life of the islands.

The Author has strong ties to this part of The Bahamas and it has been the motivating force behind the story where she was able to capture some of her childhood experiences through the eyes of the characters. Additionally, it is also her desire to share her experience during the last five years and this she hopes would be an incentive to the young people in those islands.

In the words of Susan Weyn, 'Your life is an occasion. Rise to it.' The Author is the epitome of that quotation. She rose to the changes in her life and adapted without any difficulty.

I want to commend her for finding the time despite the many diplomatic events and the usual complexities of family life to pen this story on her beloved country.

H. E. Dr. Carl Roberts CMG
High Commissioner for Antigua & Barbuda

Introduction

THE JOURNEY: An Eleuthera Experience is a family-centred historical fictional story infused with some fascinating historical details of a number of islands in The Bahamas. The story focuses on life experiences of the author, the central protagonists who decided to migrate to The Bahamas and, specifically, wanted to live in Deep Creek, Eleuthera.

Prior to leaving the United Kingdom and finalizing their plans, the adventurers, David and Laurel Thompson, both retirees, made contact with Bahama House in London, the Office of The Bahamas High Commission, to seek information and to make sure that The Bahamas was the place to re-establish their family life.

Being a diplomat and professional, the High Commissioner was delighted to share with the couple about his beloved country. Not only did he speak generally about living in The Bahamas, he gave details about his native island, Long Island, Harbour Island and mainland Eleuthera where the family wanted to go. Beaming with pride, he shared that his daughter and her family had lived in Rock Sound, Eleuthera for the past 19 years. It was his belief that the beauty and tranquillity of the Family Islands should be highlighted and shared with as many people as possible.

This story not only recounts the migration of the Thompson family but at the same time provides some history about the island they discovered and the Deep Creek Middle School. It is an independent school for students in grade seven thru nine, the equivalent of a junior high school.

Throughout the story, numerous words, name of places and expressions will be used that are more familiar with Bahamians and friends of the Bahamas for example the Glass Window bridge which connects North and Central Eleuthera, the Island School in Cape Eleuthera and Davis Harbour, a popular marina.

Additionally, the pages of this book are penetrated with information on The Bahamas as a whole; inclusive of the political, economic environment and even some social ills would be highlighted.

David and Laurel the main characters in the story felt that they were on the right track and the decision to move was the right one. They were both tired of the cold and wet weather in the UK and would miss the cultural life especially the theatre. From their internet research they believed that the tropical marine climate in The Bahamas was exactly what they were looking for.

You may guess, from the story so far that the couple were eager to leave but there was one issue to address, Susan. David and Laurel almost forgot to seek the agreement of their daughter Susan who sometimes proved a little difficult. Susan is portrayed as an emotionally trouble child, very timid, lacks confidence and can be withdrawn. Would the change in her environment create more problems for her parents?

Laurel, a strong woman in the family, is shown to be the person in charge. She is the firm parent and this was brought out quite clearly when Laurel got involved in the life of the new community and David the more laid back of the two, was satisfied staying near to home to look after the needs of their daughter Susan.

It is hoped that individuals of all ages, inclusive of young people, will find this book interesting and enlightening, especially from an historical point of view. It would give them a glimpse of life on the islands during 'yesteryears'. Additionally, the friendship that was established by Susan brings out the qualities of cheerfulness and hospitality which are pervasive attitudes not only in Eleuthera but the entire Bahamas.

For those not familiar with The Bahamas, they will enjoy discovering Eleuthera along with David and Laurel and by extension would also be made aware of the remainder of the Family Islands in The Bahamas.

Chapter 1

*T*he crystal clear blue waters, pink shimmering sand and warm climate were such enticing characteristics that David and Laurel could not resist the opportunity to relocate to The Bahamas although they had very little information about the islands.

To begin gathering information, David began by searching for the Bahamas High Commission. The research found that they were closer to the High Commission than they were aware. Therefore they immediately arranged an appointment for the next day with Mr. Paul Farquharson, the High Commissioner.

The High Commissioner, Mr. Paul Farquharson warmly greeted them, and, with formalities out of the way, David explained their reason for meeting with him. He was immediately immersed in a brief history of The Bahamas and its former ties to the United Kingdom. Not taking any chances, the High Commissioner also told Laurel and David that 'the name "Bahamas" originated from the Spanish word 'Baja mar' meaning shallow sea. High Commissioner Farquharson further shared that The Bahamas is an archipelago of over 700 Islands . . . became independent on 10 July 1973 and is now known as The Commonwealth of The Bahamas. With 325 years of British rule and over 270 years of democratic rule, The Bahamas is one of the most politically stable countries in the world'. Every five years peaceful elections are held and for the most part governance is continuous.

Noting that the island of Eleuthera was the main attraction for the couple and that they were especially interested in obtaining information about Deep Creek, the High Commissioner also mentioned the locations in Eleuthera, in which he had special interest, namely, Tarpum Bay, Eleuthera and Harbour Island. David and Laurel soon got even further insight into the wonderful Island of Eleuthera because the daughter of the High Commissioner lived in Tarpum Bay. This was good news because the couple knew they would now have friends on the Island and that whenever they visited Harbour Island they would meet relatives of the High Commissioner's wife.

Being an Ambassador, the High Commissioner earnestly encouraged David and Laurel to relocate and give The Bahamas a chance. He further shared with them that since being in the UK, he had the opportunity to speak to another couple that eventually relocated to Freeport, Grand Bahamas. He also noted that he had met other individuals who spoke of either being born in The Bahamas or having parents that had lived and even had property on some of the islands. These persons indicated their desire to one day visit and locate their inherited property.

Being pleased with their visit David and Laurel felt they had achieved a milestone.

"David, what a wonderful session we had, he was so personable and made us feel right at home", said Laurel who felt that they had made the right decision. David slightly nodding his head was already busy making mental notes of things they would have to do to achieve their goal.

After much research and discussion with friends, family and the High Commissioner, they jointly felt that the small settlement of Deep Creek, Eleuthera in The Bahamas would be the ideal location. The Commissioner shared with them the different islands and what they had to offer. They thought about them all and they decided on Deep Creek Eleuthera. Migrating to a warmer climate would be a major venture for the Thompsons. David and Laurel were happy with the island even though it was just one hundred and ten miles long and in some parts it was as little as a mile wide. They were ready for adventure and read everything they could find on the Island. They learned that the Island itself used to be thriving between 1950—1980 with dairy products, wonderful pineapples and many resorts. Unfortunately, not much was happening at this time, although some pineapples were still grown in the settlement of Gregory Town. All in all, David and Laurel believed they could adjust to the quaint community with its scattered homes among the natural foliage.

They were very eager about their decision but forgot that they had a twelve year old daughter who was very picky and perhaps saw things differently. Could she adjust to the drastic move? With much care and thought about their approach, David suggested that a good opportunity to mention the plan to their daughter would be during a visit to their friends who live near the seaside in Brighton. Although Susan loved going to the beach in Brighton, they were not able to take advantage of it very often because of the weather. Cold, damp, and rainy conditions always seemed to confront them. For this very reason, David was determined to live elsewhere but would still visit the UK periodically.

Brighton, which is one hour away by train from London, is a very touristic cosmopolitan cultural centre and was once a fishing village. The day on Brighton beach turned out to be wonderful. David and Laurel saw this as a blessing and hope to use the lovely weather to entice Susan so that she would consider the move. Looking at her enjoying the water, they realized that their task would be easy . . . or so they thought! Not long after getting started and sharing information on Eleuthera, Susan unceremoniously rejected their plan and told them she could not leave all of the friends she had made. She was by no means anxious to go to somewhere she was unfamiliar and had no friends.

Both Laurel and David were shocked and taken aback at their daughter's reaction, but they were not to be put off. They highlighted the delightful beaches on Eleuthera and that there would not be any pebbles on the beach, only pure pink sand shimmering in the dazzling sun light. They also told her that they understood her love for their weather but going to The Bahamas would offer her a better quality of life and the weather is almost perfect. There would be very little need to make use of thick over coats and that rain would be at a minimum. Even though they agreed with her that she would be leaving friends behind, they told Susan that she could also look forward to meeting new friends and cherishing the fact that she was able to share her life with them before coming to the Island. In the end, still not being satisfied, Susan told her parents that she would think about it.

Feeling relieved that they were able to share some information with Susan, David and Laurel decided to leave the matter for the time being. They realised that it would be hard on their daughter because she would be leaving the place she called home and all of her friends. Would she be able to make new friends? Since she was approaching adolescence, would she be accepted in the new school and environment? Both parents thought of their daughter's emotional well being but David, being very upbeat reassured Laurel that things would work out.

Together, the family walked out onto Brighton Pier where they were able to enjoy a seafood lunch. Both David and Laurel brought up the subject of the move again because on Eleuthera they would have fresh fish and the famous 'conch' a lovely shell fish that most tourists to the islands of The Bahamas rave about. This got Susan's attention because she never heard of this 'conch' and was intrigued when they told her that it is marinated with onions, tomatoes, pepper and lemon. Recognising that Susan never seen this shell fish, David and Laurel had a picture of the shell and shell and conch salad conch salad for her to see. Susan told her parents that she would like to taste the dish they were describing and being a fish lover, also wanted to taste fresh fish. "Wow", said David and he looked at Laurel. They continued sharing with Susan how the High Commissioner talked about the fresh fish caught daily by the fishermen in another small settlement also in Eleuthera called Tarpum Bay. This too caught Susan's attention because she commented on the strange name and asked her parents if they were aware of its meaning. Both parents were stunned because they had never thought about the meaning. However, they quickly promised that it would be an adventure, on their arrival, to seek out answers from the local community.

As they finished up their dessert and began to leave the pier, Susan focused on the merry-go-round. David and Laurel winked at each other and felt that they were making progress. This was confirmed when they over heard Susan's conversation with her friend Pamela.

"Pamela, you would never guess what my parents told me a few minutes ago. They want to relocate to an island in The Bahamas miles away from here. Girl, I don't want to go, but they have said some things that sound good" said Susan.

"You said The Bahamas . . . where in The Bahamas? I know they have many islands" said Pamela.

"Oh yes I forgot, it's the island of Eleuthera in the settlement called Deep Creek. Just the name itself put me off. I would like to go but I am scared because I would be leaving all of my friends" said Susan.

"Listen Susan, I am familiar with that island . . . my relatives visited there last year and they bragged about its beauty, especially the pink sand. Cheer up, you are up to the challenge and will certainly make new friends, my cousin still email one of the girls she met there" said Pamela.

David and Laurel were excited and walked slowly so Susan could catch up with them; however Susan made no mention of her conversation with Pamela. Not wanting to put any pressure on her they waited for Susan to come to them if she wanted to talk. Laurel very much wanted her daughter to be comfortable with the move and felt certain that she would make the right decision.

Being thrilled with what they had overheard, Susan's parents continued their plans for relocation. Information on flights from the UK and from Nassau to Eleuthera, accommodations, schools, shops, and churches were accessed via the internet and appeared to be satisfactory. A local businessman, who was recommended by the High Commissioner, Mr John Carey was also instrumental in looking at prices for purchasing a home. David and Laurel no longer needed both their homes and planned to sell the one in Mayfair so that they could purchase a new one in Deep Creek. However, they also had to consider Cape Eleuthera because of information from their salesman and over the internet; suitable accommodation may not be available in Deep Creek. They discovered that there would be shrubbery and lots of flowering plants surrounding the properties, much to the delight of Laurel.

Scattered among the homes in the town centre, they found out that there were many small stores and natives restaurants which they felt would be very convenient. This would be particularly important when they wanted to eat out and have an opportunity to meet people from the community. Sharil's Restaurant in Deep Creek was highly recommended because of the delicious cracked conch and famed as a popular eatery for tourists.

This all sounded exciting but there was still the matter of Susan. Would she inform them tonight about her decision? She was still at school and would later attended music lessons. From all indications she seemed to be more relaxed and with that kind of vibe, her parents believed that she would go along with the planned relocation date of August 1st.

But they were in for a surprise. Susan came home and went straight to her room without mentioning the move. Unfortunately for David and Laurel, Pamela had mentioned the relocation to another friend. The news spread within the class and resulted in Susan's behaviour. Susan was not prepared for the reaction of her classmates and thus became upset just as she was coming to grips with leaving the surroundings so familiar to her. Ironically, it was that blunder that ultimately pushed her to make up her mind to leave; she felt her one friend had let her down. Just before dinner she came into the TV room:

"Mum, Dad I have been thinking about what you said and I will accept the challenge of relocating" said Susan.

"That's wonderful" said her mum and of course, her father David was smiling from ear to ear.

Both parents thanked God and felt a load was removed from their shoulders because they had done a whole lot of preparation before telling Susan. Hence, they were truly disturbed when she initially verbalized her objection. Would this be the end of Susan's saga?

Chapter 2

With three weeks left prior to their date of departure, there was the packing, the collecting of school reports for Susan, the transportation arrangements and the finalizing of the house sale to be made. They had to make provisions for the dog that had been with them for many years, at one point they thought about bringing him to Eleuthera but were assured by their neighbour that they would take good care of him.

To their surprise Susan became more involved and joined in with the packers in making sure that her personal items were secured. She had many athletic trophies and other school items that she wanted to take with her.

David left the packers to Laurel and Susan while he made sure that the Estate agent was completing the paper work on the sale of the house. Besides the packers, the family also had lots of well wishers visiting despite the fact that they needed to complete their packing, especially the items to be shipped.

All too soon, that great day had arrived. The Addison Lee Cab service was on time and David, Laurel and Susan were on their way to the airport during the early morning hours to terminal five for their flight to Nassau. Not much was being said as each one got their last glimpse of Mayfair and the surrounding areas. Despite knowing that they would return, for vacations, did not make leaving any easier as they all sat in a reflective mode.

Transatlantic flights were always busy and to their surprise there were large numbers of persons travelling. This, however, could also be explained by the fact that August is traditionally the last peak month of vacation. Nevertheless, this atmosphere inspired Susan and she was very upbeat was already making friends with some of the younger passengers. That was a good sign and both David and Laurel took note of that.

Settling comfortably in business class was completed and the plane was on the runway ready for lift off. Laurel noticed that Susan appeared to be anxious; she then remembered that this would be their daughter's first transatlantic flight. Pulling out various books and playing a miniature scrabble game, soon took her mind off what was happening and she began to appreciate the flight. Once the in-flight movies began to play this too was a great help. David who also didn't like flying was enjoying his wine and most likely would be asleep even before the first meal was served.

For Laurel, she was mentally going over in her head the requirements for entry into The Bahamas and hoping that the flight would keep to the schedule. Once they landed in Nassau, the capital, they would have to take a connecting flight on Pineapple Airline to Rock Sound, Eleuthera. Susan interrupted her thoughts.

"Mum, I never told you that Pamela is not my friend any more. She was so mean to me" said Susan.

Laurel's ears perked up and she reflected on her daughter's previous behaviour.

"Mean to you, what do you mean? What happened?" her Mum replied.

"She told the whole class that I was leaving and it was not her place to do that. I felt bad about telling her off but I believed that she was out of order".

Laurel thought about what her daughter said before answering. She knew that sometimes Susan could be overbearing but agreed that Pamela was wrong for telling the class. She should have allowed Susan to tell her class mates. Most likely Susan saw it as Pamela being happy to see her leave the school.

"Susan, never mind that incident, I am sure they will miss you".

That response seems to have satisfied Susan and she immediately returned to watching the movies and tracking the plane on the map. Shortly thereafter, Laurel noted that she was fast asleep and this gave her an opportunity to complete the various forms required for immigration.

Very good, the captain had just announced that with the tail wind they were ahead of schedule and so there would be more than enough time to get to the gate for the flight to Rock Sound. David slept through the meal but was now alert and anxious to get on the ground which would be in the next thirty minutes.

Susan was awake and like her parents she hurriedly put away her book and game. Intermittently she was glancing out of the window to get her first glimpse of Nassau. There was a smooth landing and very soon they were walking toward the terminal at the Linden Pindling Airport.

The layers of clothing worn by them were shed as they walked to the terminal. Although they did not know at that time that August was one of the hottest months for The Bahamas, they found it extremely warm. They thanked God for the air-conditioning, once they got in the terminal. Clearing immigration was no problem however; they had to wait about twenty minutes for the luggage. Eventually, they made it to the other side of the terminal to a congested area where several small planes were leaving to go to one of the many Islands in The Bahamas which are locally referred to as 'Family of Islands'. Pineapple Air with its friendly staff assisted them and with several other travellers they made the twenty minute flight to Rock Sound.

The flight over to Eleuthera was smooth and the scenery was magnificent. The clear blue water and the aerial view of the entire island were wonderful. Susan's eyes were glued to the window of the plane and she continuously and gleefully shouted her amazement. Both David and Laurel were so happy with her reaction that they made the right decision when selecting their new home.

"How do you do" said John, the real estate agent.

He was able to recognize them without any difficulty because he knew almost everyone who lived in the settlement and they were the ones with the biggest smiles. He was delighted to welcome them. Seemingly, a very good natured man, he arranged transportation for them and after the collection of the bags they started their fourteen mile journey to Deep Creek. Noticeably during the drive Susan was very quiet and had a sullen look on her face. Meanwhile the drive took them through several small settlements and they also got a taste of the heat despite the fact that a mild breeze was blowing. Immediately both parents took note of Susan's change in behaviour and made eye contact with each other. They were not sure what was happening but they were soon to find out.

Chapter 3

*D*riving through a number of settlements was fascinating especially since they were not use to people waving at them in such a friendly manner. Was this an indication that life would be easy for them? All too soon they were in Deep Creek and at the home where they would reside on a temporary basis until their furniture arrived. People from the community were standing in groups watching them and those nearby greeted them with a cheery 'good afternoon'. That was a promising start for David and Laurel but they still had concerns about Susan. She said very little during the drive, and even with the friendliness of the people she was unresponsive.

"David, I hope she has not gone into her 'shell', you remember when we moved to Essex we had to have a life coach and support from a social worker to work with her for about six months. Essex was not very far and that move seem to have affected her greatly" said Laurel.

"I had been thinking the same thing Laurel, but we need to simply watch her for the time being and not even attempt to engage her in matters regarding this new community" David responded.

Very soon after entering the house and later walking in the garden, David noticed that a school was very close to the home.

"Susan" he shouted, "a school is very near and if this is Deep Creek Middle School, you would not have far to go". He was happy about seeing a school in the neighbourhood and that Susan would likely be highly motivated to attend. Previously they had concerns about her also not socializing with the other students in her former school.

"Dad that is nice but I am feeling timid" said Susan.

David recognised that his daughter was not happy at this moment and needed to get to the bottom of her discomfort. The life coach indicated that she may need further support after their sessions, but now they were in The Bahamas. Was there such a practice here? During their planning, both he and Laurel forgot about the challenge they had with Susan but this had brought back memories.

"David", called Laurel "we should walk in the community to get acquainted and to discover if there are any local food stores around to purchase food items".

David agreed and thought that this too might give him the opportunity to find out the types of social services that may be offered in the community. Together along with Susan, the family went for a walk and hoped to locate a food store. This was an eye opener for them because they learnt that the major food store was near the airport but this small shop keeper was hoping that he could provide them with the basic items until the next day. Surprisingly they got everything that was needed and had a brief chat with the shop keeper. He was friendly and wanted to know about them and what they were doing in this part of the world. Meanwhile Susan listened keenly and observed the surrounding area. There was a small park with a swing along with some children playing a jumping game in the street. Looking closer, she found out that it was a game they called 'hop-scotch' while it may have looked strange to some, the children seemed to be having fun hopping and jumping, sometimes on one leg or both. Across from there, another group was playing ball and that looked like fun too. Focusing on her parent's conversation, she realized they were making enquires about the school, whether there was a church in the community and generally getting information about their new surroundings.

The school, Deep Creek Middle School, was named for the settlement and accepted students for grades, seven to nine, and ages 11-13. Susan was beginning grade seven so obviously this would be the school she would attend. They further learnt that it was an independent school funded by a non-profit organisation—Cape Eleuthera Foundation. It was started in 2001 with thirty-five students, and from what was shared with them, the school community continued to be a small number of children.

Both David and Laurel liked that information and felt that it would be a smooth transition for Susan and her assimilation into the school setting. They were determined to put visiting the school on the top of their list because school would open in a few weeks. As for Susan, she appeared to be distant but they knew she might be experiencing fear which they hoped to alleviate once they put their plan in place.

The morning after their first night in their temporary home, Susan's face was sullen after sleeping late. She rejected all of their suggestions about how she could begin to engage with the community. David did not like these telltale signs of maladjustment. Did he regret the relocation? Not so, Susan needed more time to get acquainted with the community, especially children in her age group. A planned walk about in the settlement should cure that.

Chapter 4

While reflecting on his daughter and how quickly she had grown, David remembered last year when he sent her to life coaching classes. This came about because of her lack of motivation in the classroom and because she did not socialize as he thought she ought to have with her peers.

Both he and Laurel felt that the Life coaching six week programme followed by a six—month follow up programme was very helpful. They began to see Susan blossom into a vibrant child. Of course he thought about this because he hoped that relocation and the fact that the life coach was now many miles away was not having an impact on her life. In making the decision to move, he didn't make any inquires regarding such a service. He would have to remember to mention it when he visited the school because surely the teachers would be able to tell him if such a service was available on the island.

Since arriving in Eleuthera, Susan had been very quiet and this reflected her behaviour prior to the life coaching classes. This behaviour was of concern to David and after much discussion with Laurel; they agreed that they must be supportive while she gets over the move.

Another walk in the village further enlightened their familiarity with the settlement in particular and the island of Eleuthera in general. With the sun shining, all of them were grateful that they brought hats to shade the sun, but it would appear that their umbrellas would also help. What friendly people? Everyone greeted them with 'good morning' or a hand wave. Stopping at a store owned by Mr. Stubbs', they were welcomed. They also admired his animals:—goats and ducks—which were enclosed and walking around the yard looking very healthy. Before leaving, he let them know that it was safe to walk and explore the settlement and that they had very little crime. They were very surprised to hear that and felt even more comfortable that they had made the right decision in leaving the UK with its incidents of criminal activities and the fact that young men generally seemed to be the target.

Deep Creek Middle School was just in front of them as they walked along the main road and they were happy to go into the office to find out more about its operation. After obtaining the required forms and completing a guided tour offered by the school secretary, David, Laurel and Susan left the premises. They promised to return the forms the following day because Susan might have had to undergo an entrance test. Susan had very little to say but her parents felt it was again due to her trying to get familiar with her new surroundings. They were pleased to know that there would be small classes and that the children came from various settlements.

Their walk through the community was a social event. The people were either in their yards or sitting on the porches of their houses waiting to see who would pass. As they passed by the houses, the familiar wave and good morning greetings was repeated on every street.

Entering the Anglican Church of St. Joseph was a relief from the warm sunshine. They browsed through the small church and sat for a while. There were some ladies from the community busily cleaning and preparing for Sunday's service. Engaging them, David found out that this was voluntary and done on a weekly basis. They appeared to be quite happy mopping the floor and cleaning the candle sticks, among other tasks.

Susan commented on the size of the church and its wooden structure. This was new to her because in the UK their church structures were very large and made from bricks. Overhearing her conversation, one of the ladies told them that plans were in the making to build a stone church and asked if they were Anglicans. Their affirmation was a delight to the ladies and immediately the three ladies surrounded David, Laurel and Susan. They invited them to attend church the next day. Laurel, who normally attend church accepted their invitation and glanced at David to get his confirmation. Surprisingly, instead of David responding, Susan affirmed that she would be interested in attending. Her mother was very proud of her because previously Sunday mornings were problematic and always ended with Laurel giving in and allowing Susan to sleep in. At home in the UK, they attended the Grosvenor Chapel, which is a branch of the Church of England, but in The Bahamas it is known as the Anglican Church. Laurel was looking forward to experiencing the service in Deep Creek.

Just before ending the conversation, they asked the ladies about directions to the beach. The response was disappointing because the better or more popular beaches were in another settlement called Tarpum Bay or Rock Sound which required them to drive. Taxis were limited in the settlement and their arranged transportation would not be collecting them until the following week. They missed their car and waited anxiously for its arrival so they could readily explore their new home. They already knew that Susan wanted to see the pink beaches and taste the native conch.

The walk did the trick, Susan was talking again and her parents were happy.

Chapter 5

With breakfast completed, the family prepared to walk the short distance to the Anglican Church. Laurel was excited and looked forward to experiencing the service.

To their surprise, the church was full. They were not accustomed to that because in the UK not everyone went to church. Being visitors, they were seated at the very front which was a good place to be but David, who was not use to attending church, felt out of place. Laurel, however, did her best to put him at ease. Wow! They are having high mass despite the fact that the church was located in the tiny settlement of Deep Creek. What they found out was that it was the church's Patronal Festival and that the other sister churches came to visit for the special occasion.

Also, to their surprise the Bishop of The Bahamas, Turks and Caicos was present. This really meant so much to Laurel, as it was her family's first visit to the church. Instead of the one hour church service which they were use to in the UK, Laurel and her family spent two and a half hours in church. David whispered to Laurel about the time and hoped that it would not last much longer. Susan on the other hand was rather disappointed because there was no Sunday school, however at the end of the service she began to make friends with some of the children during the time of refreshment. David, sticking very close to Laurel, wanted to leave but didn't interrupt his wife who was engaged in conversation with the ladies. The family was fully welcomed, especially by the ladies that had invited them the previous day. Laurel found out about the Anglican Church Women (ACW) organisation, the time for Sunday school and even inquired about something for David. She knew he would not be a willing partner in the activity but hoped that since there would not be too much distraction in the settlement he would welcome the opportunity to be with other men.

Looking up from the group of women, she saw Rachel, one of her new friends bringing the Bishop to meet them. Pleasantries were exchanged and they were pleased to share with Bishop Boyd their experience at their home Church, Grosvenor Chapel. They were extremely delighted to let him know that for many years most of the High Commissioners posted to London for The Bahamas attended Grosvenor Chapel. They assisted with the Church Fair, attended church regularly, attended their special Lenten talks and services, and, most of all, participated in church outings. They also wanted to let the Bishop know that they would be supportive of this church and looked forward to fully engaging with the congregation. They also met Rev. Bradley Miller, who was recently ordained. He is serving at Christ the King Church in Nassau. Rachel, a faithful member of the church was happy to share this achievement with them. She also mentioned how the members of the church encouraged him in pursuing his career.

Catching up with Susan after the service, they were introduced to two of her new friends. George appeared to be shy and Janae who was very bubbly wanted to know more about where they came from. David immediately felt that she would be good for Susan but was not too sure about George. Ah, but George may not be so shy after all thought David. After being introduced to Susan's parents, he left quietly and soon returned with his parents, who to David and Laurel's surprise had also relocated to Deep Creek, from the United States. Susan and her parents realized that this had accounted for the difference in his accent. George's parents were delighted to meet them and filled them in very quickly on some of the areas that they might like to visit; and extended an invitation for them to also visit their home.

It was 1pm when they returned home from church. While walking they all agreed that the church service was truly a social event in the community. Not only did they see this in regard to the Anglican Church but all other churches in the community were also seen to have a goodly number of persons in attendance. They also noticed that shops and bars were closed and there seemed to be quietness about the community. Later they found out that this was the way the community observed their Sundays, shops do not open. What a contrast from where they came from? However, both David and Laurel had no problem with it. Being avid readers, they spent the rest of the day on the back porch reading and enjoying the balmy breeze. Laurel was happy that they ate the various snacks offered at Church and she did not have to hurry to cook the evening meal.

Feeling refreshed after a relaxing evening David, Laurel and Susan set off in a different direction from their previous stroll, to further explore the settlement. They walked as far as Delancy Town and were able to see where the local clinic was located in addition to a small government primary school. They again noticed the friendliness of the people who wanted to engage in conversation with them and to learn where they came from.

On the walk, David pointed out to Laurel and Susan the low lying land and the fact that they could see the blue waters of the sea. He also showed them the mangroves along the shore line. For David, Laurel and Susan it was a pleasant sight and a relaxing walk. They were not accustomed to leisure walking due to the weather in the UK and being so far inland there was usually no way for them to see the sea unless they visited a coastal town.

Susan who was walking jauntily, slightly ahead of her parents seemed to have forgotten her fears and accepted her new surroundings. Laurel was extremely proud of her but David kept remembering her remarks about being timid and still felt that they needed to find out if there was a life coach in the community.

Returning home and after supper, Laurel settled down to read her book while David watched television. Susan wanted to go on the porch to watch the children who may be playing in the street. She soon realized that there were children but not playing as they did the day before. They were dressed in nice clothing and visiting neighbours. George stopped by and told her that this was something that was done every Sunday after Sunday school. Well that was new to her but nevertheless she stayed on the porch watching the children all dressed up walking down the street. Some of them remembered seeing her and gave the usual hand wave.

Oops! No lights! David, Laurel and Susan were disturbed by this. No one told them to expect this. Candles and matches were nowhere to be found, but there was a knock on the door and a familiar voice of the real estate agent John greeted them. He was in the neighbourhood and recognized that they may not have a lantern and kerosene oil required to light the Lantern. They were happy to see him and all of them began to talk about the power outage. Meanwhile he showed them how to light the lantern and informed them that from time to time there are outages but they don't last for long periods. Before John left, a few of the neighbours also came to the home to ensure that the newcomers were doing okay. David and Laurel was surprise by the generosity and the good nature of the community and truly felt that they were among friends. With nothing much to do after the power outage, they talked among themselves about the experience so far. Susan emphasised that she wanted to go to the beach, taste the marinated conch and go to a big food store. Would she get her wish?

Chapter 6

M onday morning was bright and sunny. David was on the porch looking out for the car to take them to Rock Sound and the surrounding settlements. They planned to spend the day exploring that part of the island and would hopefully get to do some of the things Susan requested.

Travelling along the road into Rock Sound, the family admired the lovely blue waters which they saw periodically and responded eagerly to the waves of the native community. They drove pass the Market Place food store and decided not to stop but to leave that as their last stop. They continued on to Tarpum Bay where they passed the famous Columbo Anglican Church usually featured in magazines worldwide, prior to stopping at the Fish dock.

Susan was excited when she saw a group of children fishing. This was an experience she was not familiar with. Besides, the sea water in this new home was much better than what she was used to. Unfortunately, the fishermen were still out to sea but further down the road there was a conch vendor and they were able to get conch for Susan. It was spicy and they quickly had to find a store to get some water for her to drink. With tears streaming down her face she expressed her dismay at the taste and wanted to know if that was always the case. David and Laurel were grimacing to each other so that she would not see them fill of laughter. Their daughter was so eager to eat conch she did not pay attention to the details regarding the fact that it was a spicy dish. Lucky for them, Carey's Food Fair was nearby and they all got a cool drink. The shopkeeper was pleased to have them at the store and greeted them in a lively Tarpum Bay accent. They found out that he was Mr. Carey who gladly told them a bit of history on the settlement. He pointed out the primary school and was happy to say that all of his children attended that school. Later on, he showed them the other part of the store that belonged to his brother and he was quick to point out that if they needed any appliances that store—Buy Wise Hardware—was the place to go. That was of interest to David and Laurel because they needed some appliances. They did not ship those items because those made in the UK were not compatible with the electricity in The Bahamas. They promised Mr. Carey that they would return as soon as they moved into their home.

Mr. Carey also thought it important to tell David and his family about Lord McMillan Hughes, who most likely came from the UK. He was a premier artist and many of his works are displayed around Tarpum Bay and the other settlements. The Hughes Castle was very big and dominated the townscape in the settlement and this caused David to truly believe that he must have been English because such 'castles' are popular in the UK.

While returning to their car, they met a young man and his family. James welcomed them to Tarpum Bay and shared with them places of interest where they could find good Bahamian food. He stressed that their driver should take them to 'Tippy's' and they would have an opportunity to get a glimpse of the pink sand and if the water was not to rough they could even get a dip in the water. This was good news for Susan because she was waiting patiently to put her feet in the water. Before leaving with his wife, Vonnette and their three children, James also told them about Sammy's Restaurant in Rock Sound. While visiting this establishment they would also get a firsthand look at the interior of Rock Sound; getting a look at how the community lived. Of course he did not forget to tell them to visit the blue hole which is an historical site in Rock sound.

While driving out of Tarpum Bay the Driver drove into a small motel called Ingraham's Beach Inn and there, David, Laurel and Susan were able to get their first glimpse of the pink sand. He told them that on the Atlantic side of the island, the pinkness would be even more pronounced. There were 'ahs' and 'wows' coming from the family. They were sure amazed at the beauty because up to that point in their lives, they were used to seeing very coarse, dark coloured sand along with pebbles on their beaches. Dipping their feet in the clear blue waters, they spoke to each other about the warmth and mentioned that they could not wait to be totally immersed in the water. That experience was the topic during most of the drive until the driver shared with them a myth about the three mile stretch of road where a ghost gets into the car and begins talking. They laughed almost hysterically. Susan laughed but also got very serious and wanted to know if there was any truth to the story. David very quickly took control and she was comforted knowing that it was just a tale which is usually shared with visitors to the community and not to worry.

The trip was planned for as far as Savannah Sound which was thirty miles from Deep Creek to collect some homemade bread. This was cut short when they decided they needed to eat. After hearing about Sammy's, they wanted to try his food and so they returned to Rock Sound and ate at that restaurant. On this occasion Susan tried the cracked conch and fries while her parents tried stew fish. These were all unusual dishes for them but the driver encouraged them to give it a try. To his surprise and theirs, they enjoyed their meal and rounded off with guava duff which is like a jelly roll in the UK. The dessert captured their attention and they reminisced and compared it to their bread and butter pudding which they had in the UK. The scrumptious food continued to be the topic of their conversation during the drive to the Market Place Food store to do their grocery shopping.

The trip to the grocery store was an experience and it took longer than expected because they were busy reading every canned item and trying to find foods that were familiar to them. With some luck and with the Market Place importing foods from a variety of suppliers, they were satisfied that their food items were good and not too far off from what they normally found in the food stores in the UK.

Both David and Laurel sighed with contentment as they continued the journey home. They could now have a proper home cooked meal and truly feel at home in their new surroundings. To their delight, a large bowl of mixed vegetables greeted them as they entered the porch with a note from their neighbour. This was their way of welcoming new families to the community. This gesture really made their day and David later told Laurel that they made the right choice of coming to live in Eleuthera.

With the meal cooking and each of them into their favourite book, George and Janae knocked on the door. They came to spend some time with Susan who was eager for their company and to share with them her morning experience. Of course, Janae were very familiar with the island and George having been there for about two years was knowledgeable as well. Nevertheless, they listened and were just as happy as Susan as she told her story. Their attention turned to the upcoming school year and they were both happy to know that Susan would be joining them at the Deep Creek Middle School. They told her about the bus route and where she could get the bus if her parent's car didn't arrive before the opening. They noticed that Susan became quiet while they shared this information. David heard them pleading with her and realized something was wrong. Yes, something was wrong; her face said it all when he appeared at the porch door. Quickly he told the friends that she was tired and they left for home but not before glancing back at the porch to see what was going on. Susan was hugging her father and looked like she was crying. George and Janae was really concerned and wondered if they had upset Susan.

Fear gripped Susan and she held tightly on to her daddy. Going to school created the fear and with teary eyes Susan told her daddy what George and Janae had said about catching the bus to school. This episode reinforced David's effort to find a life coach or social worker to acquaint them with Susan's emotional history and for them to begin to build a relationship. There is no doubt that during the first few months on the island she would require some help.

Laurel announced that the meal was ready and this is when she became aware that Susan was going through a challenging moment. David did a fine job of comforting and reassuring her that school would be fine when she began the school year. Susan already had two good friends and they would help her to meet other new students and she knew that her daddy would go with her on the first day. That reassurance and a hug from her mother brought a smile to her face and they settled to have their meal, the first one cooked in the home. They were happy to be sitting in their own living room instead of in a restaurant.

Shortly after completing the meal, there was another knock on the door. It was John, the real estate agent. He had come to inform them that within fourteen days he would be receiving word from the lawyers concerning the purchase of their home, and also that the G & G Shipping Company traced their packages and expected it would be another six weeks before they arrive in Eleuthera. They were happy about the progress of the house but the late arrival of furniture, and the car, was disappointing. Arrangements would have to be made to rent a car, especially with school opening so soon and the fact that Susan had already shown some reservation about riding the bus. David also immediately put this on his agenda. Seeing that taxis were scarce, would he even be able to rent a car?

Chapter 7

*T*he new school term began. David along with Laurel went with Susan to her new school. Upon arrival they saw George and Janae who both waved at Susan and pointed the family in the direction of the office. Susan's transfer and report card had been sent from her school in the UK. However, when they arrived at the office, they were told that there were no report card or transfer documents for Susan.

"There must be some mistake" David whispered to Laurel while the assistant administrator was hastily going through a bunch of papers. Susan was following this activity as well and was questioning her dad who tried to smooth over what was happening. The gathering of the children on the basket ball court soon got her attention and she saw George lining up with the other children.

After a few minutes of looking through papers, they were called into the principal's office and the misplaced documents were located. They were happy to learn that Susan would be entering the seventh grade and joining thirteen other children from the surrounding settlements. The small class size was appealing to David and laurel and this was one of the reasons why David and Laurel liked the school. Additionally, they had read on the internet that the school provides a nurturing community that engages students with opportunities to learn in and out of the classroom. Inclusive in the programme were critical thinking, problem solving, interpersonal, intrapersonal and communication skills development.

Leaving Susan at the school, David and Laurel slowly drove back to their home but dare not go anywhere in the event they got a call from the school. They both relaxed around the house catching up on their reading. David was happy to read the Eleuthera newspaper which gave updates on events in each settlement. There was an article on 'Back to the Bay', a Tarpum Bay festival held on the first Monday in August. He made a mental note of that event for the following year. The Guardian newspaper one of the leading papers in Nassau was filled with political news. He learnt that The Bahamas was getting ready for their general election which occurs every five years and from all indications this one seemed to be very contentious. Although there were two major parties there were a number of small parties, some of whom had merged with the major parties, and others that wanted to remain separate and try their hand at the election. Judging from his reading and talk from the local residents elections were exciting times. David had even heard them mention what good times they have at rallies.

This was new to David and he would definitely attend whenever one was held in Eleuthera.

Laurel interrupted David's reading because she forgot to tell him that a Mrs. Forbes, the local social worker had called. She left the emotional wellbeing of Susan to him because it pained her to see that there were times when her baby seemed to be so fragile. This was good news to David because he had been trying to reach Mrs. Forbes but understood that she was in Nassau. She had recently graduated with a degree in Social work but had limited experience. He was not too happy with that news because he felt she may have been too inexperience but his fears were very soon laid to rest. A reliable source had informed him that Mrs. Forbes had, in fact, been practicing for years but recently went to Nassau, and attended the College of The Bahamas to obtain her degree. He recognised that, if anything, she should be commended for what she had done, knowing that she had to up root her family to make such a sacrifice. He was looking forward to meeting her and to seeing what plans they could develop together to ensure that Susan's transition to the settlement of Deep Creek was successful.

Meanwhile they were happy to recognise that it was already lunch time and there had been no phone call from the school. This gave them both confidence that their daughter had settled into the school environment. No longer feeling anxious about Susan's first day at school, they loafed in the warm sunshine and strolled into the community where there were several persons sitting under the big tree and others doing their washing and generally relaxing. Laurel observing the community commented to David that it was the tranquil atmosphere that drew her to the Deep Creek. The friendliness and the fact that they can walk and talk with persons on the street were lovely. Nina, one of the ladies from church was pushing her granddaughter in a stroller and was happy to see them. David and Laurel both had a chance to cuddle the baby. They invited Nina to visit them the following morning and immediately Laurel began to think about preparing English bread and butter pudding for the occasion.

Stopping at Sharil's they ordered a crack conch to share. To their surprise they did not have to wait as long as they did on their initial introduction to that restaurant. It was delicious and they commended the cook on such a well prepared dish and looked forward to returning.

A big hug and kiss was given to Susan from her parents when they collected her from school. She made the full day and there were no complaints. She was bubbling over with excitement because she liked her teacher, she liked her class mates and she was able to see Janae and George during the lunch break. She was happy to meet a teacher who was also from the UK. After bringing her parents up to date on the school activities for the first day, Susan told them she wanted to go and watch George and Janae play a game of rounders. This was a popular ball game played by the children in the settlement and when told about it Susan was anxious to learn the game. Being very protective at first, David and Laurel were reluctant. However, the look on Susan's face caused them to soften and they allowed her to go.

No sooner had they agreed George was at the door to collect her. They looked with pride at their daughter has she ventured out on her own, which was unusual due to her present emotional state. They were not altogether convinced that she had recovered but planned to walk to the ball field themselves once the game got started and, if possible, stay out of her sight so they would not spoil her fun.

During dinner, the conversation centred on the ball game including the fact that Susan believed that she could play the game well. She also met so many other children. Of course these children were curious about her back ground and where she came from, why she was in Deep Creek and about her parents. The greatest interest among the children was the difference in skin colour. Being Bahamians the children had darker skin and Susan's skin was lighter. This is intriguing for both the local children and Susan.

David and Laurel were left shock, surprise and excited as they listened to their daughter. She was very relaxed as she talked to them and there was no sign of her troubled past. More and more they were feeling that they may not need the social worker after all.

Exhausted, tired and sleepy from the day's event, Susan went to bed early. This gave David and Laurel an opportunity to reflect on the day's events. They truly felt at home and more and more knew they made the right decision particularly when considering Susan and her challenges. The change, they believed would give her a wider view on life and it definitely would not hurt her as she developed into a young adult.

With Nina being their first house guest the following day, would Laurel's preparation be successful?

Chapter 8

With Susan settled in school, David and Laurel were once again free to explore their new surroundings and on weekends they included Susan. In the morning they planned to visit the Deep Creek Sand Bar right after having mid morning tea with Nina. Laurel had already made the bread and butter pudding and was looking forward to having a visitor. For them both it was good to invite persons to their home; it also allowed them to get to know more about the settlement and aid them in integrating with the community.

Nina arrived on time and they had a splendid morning sharing and getting to know about each other. Nina, a retired school teacher was able to give David and Laurel more insight into the local educational system and they found that there were many similarities with the UK. Of course they should have expected that because The Bahamas is part of the Commonwealth and still recognised the Queen as its Head of State.

David and Laurel were able to tell Nina all about how the Queen interacted with residents at least three times a year by having three garden parties in London and three in Scotland. Roughly eight thousand people attend those functions inclusive of the Diplomatic Corp—Ambassadors and High Commissioners of the Commonwealth. It was an event where persons in attendance would be formally dressed and Diplomats, in particularly, had the opportunity to meet the Queen personally in her Tent or as the English would say in her marquee. Hors d'oeuvres would be served, including the traditional cucumber sandwiches, among others, and various pastries. These parties, they further explained took place in the summer months during June or July and in August in Scotland. Nina was excited to hear about this but also saddened that David and Laurel never had an opportunity to be invited. Nina, nevertheless appreciated that within a country of sixty million people, the selection of just a few to have this opportunity must be difficult. After almost two hours of chatting, they promised to meet again. Nina offered to host the meeting. Laurel, in particular, looked forward to the occasion because she was anxious to see how people actually lived in the settlement.

Following Nina's visit, David and Laurel went to the Deep Creek Sand Bar, which was an awesome sight. The tide was low and David and Laurel were able to walk quite a distance and feel the shimmering pink sand beneath their feet. They were however mindful of the strong sun rays and did not venture to far before returning to the car. With the whole day before them and with the help of information they had received from Nina they decided to revisit their attempt to drive to Savannah Sound to get some of the local homemade bread. The journey was pleasant. David recognised that they had taken one direct road and he had to be careful of the curves and gentle hills along the way. There was a nice breeze coming off of the sea combined with the melodious songs on the national radio station ZNS 1540. They had just missed a talk show hosted by Chrissie Love. They liked what they heard and promised to remind each other to tune in the following day because they both were very health conscious and she had mentioned something about a green smoothie.

Following the instructions given by Nina, they arrived at the home of Mr. Henry Sands who had been baking bread for many years. Previously his wife was also involved but unfortunately she passed away and now his daughter assisted him. History has it that Mr. Sands baked bread for Prince Charles and Lord Mount Batten during their visits to Windermere Island. He was even invited to London for Prince Charles first wedding. The smell of the freshly baked bread was divine and the loaves and rolls looked absolutely delicious. Being two new customers coming to purchase bread, Mr. Sands readily engaged David and Laurel in conversation. When he heard they were from London, he shared his London experience with them. By the time they left they were thrilled to have such a vibrant and energetic senior citizen, and, one who, from all accounts, was upstanding in his community. They too wanted to tell him about their experience with the recent royal wedding of Kate and Will, now known has the Duke and Duchess of Cambridge. They proceeded to share that they were with the campers on the greens. They also went on to speak about their meeting with the High Commissioner for The Bahamas to London, and he and his wife, together with the Prime Minster and his wife, and the Governor General of the

Bahamas and his wife were the six persons from The Bahamas who were privileged to be in attendance. What a story! Even as they shared those experiences they were happy reminiscing of the wedding and saw that Mr. Sands appeared to be reliving those years so long ago when he was invited to the wedding of Prince Charles and the late Princess Diana.

On their return journey home David and Laurel decided to make a stop in Tarpum Bay to the Carey's Gas Station and in addition to getting petrol, they also were introduced to sugar apples and sapodillas. These were fruits that they were certainly not familiar with but, after sampling them they were happy to buy some to take home. Additionally, Mr. Eugene Carey also had fresh vegetables from his very own farm and they purchased some of the items. They found the prices very reasonable. Feeling pleased with their purchases, David and Laurel continued their drive home and looked forward to collecting Susan from school.

How wonderful for them in that Susan's friendship with George and Janae had blossomed and she seem to have been accepted in the community of her peers.

Chapter 9

*I*t seemed like a long time since they had left London but, at last, word came that the family's few items of furniture, remaining luggage and car, would be arriving within the week. All three of them were overjoyed because they longed to be comfortable in their new home with their own furnishings. Unfortunately, this meant leaving the Deep Creek community which they had come to love.

The house became a bee hive of activity as they packed up their clothing and prepared to locate near to the Cape about ten to fifteen minutes drive from their current location.

What a lovely townhouse it was, and to their joy it was right near the water edge of Cape Eleuthera Marina. Right away they began to include their personal items among the beautiful wicker furniture that came with the home. Additionally, the decor made up of lots of hanging pictures, green foliage and bouquets on the tables all made the interior of the new home very, very attractive. Susan was happy, jumping from room to room squealing with delight about finally moving into what she could call her own.

Already she was shouting to her parents about having some of the children from Deep Creek visit and play what was now her favourite game—rounders.

After repositioning the furniture, putting away clothing and other necessary items Laurel was satisfied and later that evening was able to relax and admire the wonderful sunset. Their town house was situated in such a way that each day ended with them viewing the sunset overlooking this sparkling clear blue water whether upstairs or down stairs. David was delighted, stretched off with a wine glass of Genesis, a restorative drink like wine but without the alcohol. As far as he was concerned the trip, the wait for their personal items and the car were all worth it. What a relief! That night they slept soundly and looked forward to fully engaging in their new home.

House warming parties were nothing new to David and Laurel. They were more convinced that they needed to have one. There were many references made to their new home by the friends they had already made in the Deep Creek community. Everyone was so happy to know that at long last they were in their home, thus hinting that a party should be forthcoming. Even Susan came home from school telling them her friends were asking when the party would be. With such expectations David and his family did not want to disappoint all those persons who had treated them so well when they first arrived in the settlement. So, with the help of the Administrator at the resort, they planned the event for October 12th which was a holiday—Columbus Day. What a wonderful event it was and they were happy to see Nina, their former driver and members of the church. It was like a reunion. Additionally, their new found neighbours were also invited and later shared how thrilled they was to be a part of the celebration, an event that went on well into the evening. Susan invited all of her school mates who came in their swim wear. This group truly enjoyed themselves and Susan, in particular, was thrilled to show off her new diving skills. David and Laurel found out from this event that young people ate lots of food while the adults drank mostly alcoholic beverages. A mental note was made of this because they planned to have more parties, especially during the Christmas and New Year holidays.

At mid night the last guest left and by that time David and Laurel surely needed their bed. Shortly after nine Susan retired and was asleep almost immediately. Luckily for all of them the following day was Saturday and they could lie in.

After a late breakfast, David and Laurel reflected on the wonderful house warming gifts that they had received. Such gifts were not expected but David and Laurel were grateful because some of them were genuine island made products, items they would always cherish. It was 1 o'clock pm when Susan finally appeared but in a very sullen mood. She ate very little lunch and went off onto the porch by herself. Susan was in another one of her moods but the first since they had been in the new home and both parents became very concerned. They intended to watch her and see whether she would 'snap out of it'. Sunday morning arrived and there was no improvement. Susan wouldn't get out of bed to eat nor did she want to go to church. Laurel went to church and left David to deal with Susan. This time he tried all kinds of tactics to get her to talk about what was happening but she remained tight—lipped and slept most of the day. Later in the afternoon she had some juice, sat on the porch but said very little. The following day was school, and because she loved it, it was hoped she would be up—beat, but to David and Laurel's disappointment there was no improvement. Getting Susan out of bed for school was a chore and she finally got there but was still very sullen and near tears.

With this challenge staring them in the face their plan to visit Tarpum Bay for fish was put on hold. It was good that they remained at home. At 11:30 am, just before Susan was due to break for lunch the school rang suggesting that she be collected because she spent the whole morning with her head on the desk and was not her usual self.

David and Laurel collected Susan and they went directly to Mrs. Forbes' office in Rock Sound. They had notified her of their concern and she was there to greet them. What a pleasant greeting she gave Susan although you would not think so from Susan's expression. Nevertheless, she took her into the interviewing room and there they talked for at least an hour. Meanwhile David and Laurel thought over all the other occasions when they had to get assistance for their daughter. She seemed to lack confidence and they were never certain when an issue or an incident would create a problem for her and she would find it difficult to overcome the obstacle. In the past she had seen several persons in the caring profession and all had said that it would be something she would eventually out grow. They were praying that she would soon move beyond this part of her development.

The door opened and Mrs. Forbes requested that they join the session. What a relief! They entered the room and there was Susan with telltale signs of having been crying but still with a happy face. Being prompted by the social worker, Susan was able to verbalize her feelings and from her account of events, some of the children at the house warming party were not very nice and she felt hurt because it was her family's house celebration and she had invited them to it. David and Laurel were upset but at the same time happy that Mrs. Forbes was able to get to the bottom of what were happening. They now had their smiling daughter back again and before leaving Mrs. Forbes suggested that they bring her the following week for a follow up appointment. Mrs. Forbes' analysis characterised Susan as a timid and sometimes fearful child who could easily be intimidated, for this reason Mrs. Forbes felt that further sessions would help her gain the confidence that she needed especially given that she was still adjusting to her new home environment. She was not too sure if David and Laurel recognised that Susan was struggling to fit into the Eleuthera community although she was evidently trying extremely hard to do so.

David and Laurel were pleased that Mrs. Forbes got some results and they assured her that they would keep the next week's appointment. Susan's latest jovial mood spilled over to them and rather than going back to the Cape, the family went for an evening drive exploring more of Tarpum Bay. While out, they got invited to the Methodist Church. They had no problem with that because they were still trying to fit into a local Church.

Visiting the settlement of Tarpum Bay gave the family a completely different view. They realized the community was not just on the shore road where the nice clear blue water was inviting, but beyond it was the actual settlement where most of the residents lived. There was a spa for the locals and visitors. This was good news for Laurel because she loved to relax at a spa. Again they also noticed that warm friendly environment with which she had become so familiar from visits other parts of the island of Eleuthera. Susan saw some of her school friends that travelled the long distance between Tarpum Bay and Deep Creek to get to school. They were pleased to see her and wanted her to get out of the car and walk along with them. Seeing the eagerness on her face, her parents parked the car on a side street and they strolled the narrow winding streets, stopping periodically to talk with some of the residents. They were thrilled because it helped them to adjust not only to where they lived but get to know the island in general. What a happy family they were and they truly loved their choice of relocation.

Chapter 10

Where did the time go? Susan had completed her first year at the Deep Creek Middle School and was preparing to travel to the UK to see her grandparents. David and Laurel had one of their quarrels because David felt that their trip to the UK should be during the latter part of July as he wanted to be in The Bahamas for the Independence celebrations. His plan was to spend that time in Nassau so they could go to Ft. Charlotte and see the fireworks. Laurel misunderstood what he requested of her and made the reservations for early July. With voices raised they both tried to state how the mix up came about. In the end Laurel was left feeling really sad. David muttered under his breath but realized nothing could be done unless they decided to pay the difference for changing the tickets. In the end Laurel reminded him that they had many more years to see the celebrations because The Bahamas was now their new home. David's mood changed when he listened to his wife's soft voice.

Their arrival in the UK was met with rain and cool weather but they welcomed the change, and as Susan said to them, she was happy for the cool weather when considering the warm temperature in Eleuthera. They immediately settled in and began to plan their activity for the four week period. On top of Laurel's agenda were attendance at her beloved Grosvenor Chapel on Sunday and a mid-day service at St. James' Church, Piccadilly. St James' Anglican Church welcomes and celebrates human diversity—including spirituality, ethnicity, gender and sexual orientation. She fondly remembered those days of sitting meditating while waiting for the clergy to arrive. There was even one occasion when there was a mix up and no clergy showed up. The crisis was averted thanks to a Lay Reader who was not an ordained minister; graciously lead the Morning Prayer for those who were waiting.

Between the visits to relatives and friends, they wanted to take Susan to the London Eye, go to Harrods and most of all go across to Paris and Belgium. They also had to accommodate Susan's friends who telephoned frequently and often wanted her to go out with them. They were not pleased with those requests, especially after seeing those friends in person. What a difference one year had made. These friends of Susan, although still in their early teens, appeared somehow to be older. There was a lot of body piercing and they just looked unseemly when compared to the new friends she made in The Bahamas. A few of them were even smoking. This behaviour definitely alerted David and Laurel and they were not inclined to allow their daughter, to be in their company unchaperoned. Susan certainly did not mind not going out with them and of course Laurel saw that as a blessing in disguise.

Mayfair had not changed, very quiet on weekends and extremely busy through the week and they found themselves caught up in the fast pace all over again. The experience in Eleuthera however, allowed them to see that there could be a slower pace in the world where life could be enjoyed to the fullest without rushing. They both appreciated their work lives but now had an even better appreciation for solitude, the roaring of the ocean in stormy times and the gentle waves and sea breeze. They thought of going to Brighton but after what they had enjoyed in The Bahamas, it no longer had an appeal.

A surprise telephone call from an old friend in Bristol gave them a scare. His wife was not doing so well but they recognised that he too was showing signs of aging. These friends were actually friends of Laurel's parents, when they were alive, and periodically they rang up. They were happy to hear David and Laurel had relocated to The Bahamas and were able to give them contact information for two of their friends who lived in Nassau. Cornelius lived in Lyford Cay and Michele lived on West Bay Street. Laurel and David had little experience with Nassau but promised to look them up whenever they were there. They liked the gesture because it would help them to get acquainted with Nassau and maybe spend some time there in the not too distant future. Meanwhile they wished them both well and hope to hear from them on their next visit.

All too soon they had completed their agenda and, within days, would be heading back to The Bahamas, the place they now called home. Before leaving they graciously invited some of their friends to join them.

Much to their delight, Janet, from Grosvenor Chapel, expressed her interest in visiting The Bahamas, but wanted to go to Grand Bahama. She had heard about it from a friend and via the internet she learnt more and felt that she would want to go there. David, who was familiar with the process, shared with her what was necessary and deeply believed that the next time they heard from her she would be well on her way to relocating to that island. This was not a problem for them; they would simply not only have Nassau to visit but also Freeport, Grand Bahama. More and more people, who could afford to relocate from the UK, were selecting warmer climates.

An invitation from the Bahamas High Commission brought excitement to the home. Laurel had been invited to morning tea in honour of the Governor General's wife. They were visiting from The Bahamas and because they too had previously been in the same post, the wife of the current High Commissioner thought it fitting to invite a few friends in for tea.

"A tea party", repeated Laurel. "I have never been in such company. Was there a dress code? David I have nothing to wear. You know we came on holiday and only brought casual wear".

"Laurel that's no problem, go out and buy an outfit. You deserve it anyway, especially since we have been in Eleuthera, you did not buy any clothing" said David.

What a relief. Laurel felt better because she had David's approval to shop. Since relocating they had been somewhat frugal because of the system of getting money to Eleuthera, but that would no longer be a problem. Although there is no bank at the Cape they had opened an account at Scotia Bank in The Market Place shopping centre in Rock Sound.

The day of the tea party arrived and Laurel walked the one block to 11 Chesterfield Street where the event was being held. Being the second person to arrive, she met the hostess and was soon introduced to other ladies who were gathering in reception where they signed the official guest book while awaiting the arrival of the guest of honour. Meanwhile she met Pauline, the spouse of the Antiguan High Commissioner and they chatted awhile before being joined by Ruth, the High Commissioner for Grenada. Laurel was happy to meet persons from The Bahamas; there was Isabella, the Personal Assistant to the Director of The Bahamas Maritime Authority office, Valerie from the Tourism office, Evanya from the Bahamas High Commission office and Duchez, a Bahamian Designer. They shared with her their experiences in the UK and were even more surprised when she told them she had relocated to Cape, Eleuthera. They found it amazing and all took the opportunity to tout the beauty of the Bahama Islands.

Shortly afterwards the guest of honour arrived. Everyone was invited to the second floor into a large dining room with a lovely decorated table set for about twenty persons. The atmosphere was very lively and those who previously knew the guest of honour were happy to see her and catch up on what she had been doing since she left the UK. What a grand affair. The waiters were attentive and the selection of sandwiches, dainty cakes, scones and fruits were pleasing to the eye. New friendships were made and old ones were re-established and at the end of the tea party lots of positive comments were made, particularly about the fashion show because no one expected to be entertained so lavishly. There were models who wore lovely dresses by Yemi Osunkoya, a Designer who was on hand to explain the designs and of course also attempting to encourage new customers. He was a London—based designer specialising in contemporary and elegant bridal, evening and formal day wear that uses luxurious fabrics and sumptuous embellishment'. Laurel found out that Yemi was an 'award-winning designer who makes the dreams of his clients come true'.

Laurel was amazed and felt that it was an event that would remain with her for some time. All too soon it came to a close and individuals began to leave shortly after the guest of honour was collected by her driver. Her only disappointment was that she did not get a chance to see the High Commissioner and tell him how they had settled in Eleuthera.

Back at their home in the UK David and Susan were waiting for her wanting to hear the details of the event. When told about the fashion show both of them were enthralled. Susan wanted a description of the dresses and David expressed surprise at the event taking place at a tea party.

"Well Laurel you can truly talk about the tea party when you return to Eleuthera. Do you think we might host one there?" David remarked.

Laurel was not too certain because for the UK morning tea gatherings were part of the culture and she was not sure if there was such a custom in The Bahamas.

With their vacation coming to an end, the last few days were spent visiting David's parents in Essex and sightseeing at the London Eye and at Harrods. To David, they all seemed to be in high spirits and happy to know that they would soon be making the return journey to their new found home. Susan, who was extremely jolly collected small items to take back to George and Janae, obviously those two persons were important to her.

The family flew on Virgin Airline and stopped over for two days in Miami before the onward journey to Nassau. They had never been to Florida and with Susan being part of their decision making process, it was agreed that they would extend the holiday by two days. The flight was great and they were delighted to stay at Court Yard, a small hotel operated by Marriot, located in Miami Lakes. The hotel was a quiet area close to the shopping mall which they were able to visit. Although they got lost on many occasions and had to remember to stay on the right side of the street when driving, it was a wonderful trip for them. They promised that they would visit again and stay longer.

While in Miami, they met up with Valerie Mathias who invited them to her Church—Saint Agnes, which had a Bahamian connection. They learnt that the church Priests had Bahamian roots. The current one was preparing to retire and already there was talk to replace him with a Priest from The Bahamas.

Additionally, they later learnt from the internet that 'Bahamians who moved to Miami to establish new lives for themselves started the nucleus of the church. When they lived in The Bahamas many of them were members of St. Agnes in Grant's Town, thus the group name their new church St. Agnes'.

Laurel who always expressed her love for worshiping was enthused and mentioned to David that she would share the information with Nina and Rachel when they returned home.

Travelling to Nassau on Bahamasair, they marvelled at the tranquil waters and the fact they flew over Andros Island. Connecting with Pineapple Air was no problem; they certainly had sufficient time but when they arrived they did not get a single piece of their luggage.

"Laurel, we need to speak to someone to arrange to have the luggage sent to us in Eleuthera" stated David.

Spotting an agent in the distance they spoke to him and the situation was quickly sorted out. They were still very disheartened because like all travellers they wanted and expected their luggage to arrive with them. The agent assured them however that it should be on the next flight. Would they be lucky to get their luggage?

Chapter 11

*P*ineapple Airline, as usual, was on time and they were soon airborne. Both Laurel and David had been nodding when they were alerted to an announcement coming from the pilot. Their plane was being diverted to North Eleuthera, miles away from the Rock Sound's Airport, where they were schedule to land. Further information revealed that there would be buses to take them to Rock Sound. Shortly afterwards, they landed at the North Eleuthera Airport and marvelled at the surroundings. There were a few tourist shops across the street and even a small cafe and restaurant. They learnt that this airport covered the north of the island. Laurel recalled seeing information on this section on the internet while she was researching the facts about Deep Creek. While sharing the information with David they had always planned to visit, so this unforeseen stop gave them a bird's eye view of that part of the island. From the history of the island they were familiar with its farming capability and it was inclusive of Harbour Island and Spanish Wells. A brief conversation with Limon, a taxi driver 'wet' their appetite and they told him they would be back sooner than they had planned.

Despite the inconvenience of being on this part of the island, Laurel and her family were thankful that they had arrived back safely and looked forward to the drive to Rock Sound. On the bus there was James who they previously met in Tarpum Bay. He became their personal guide because Limon although very friendly, had to keep his eyes on the road and was not able to help as much as he wished.

Whale Point and Bottom Harbour were the first places highlighted and they were encouraged to visit a small restaurant in that area whenever they return. They heard tales of how that was the nearest point to Harbour Island and in the past, persons from Harbour Island used to travel that way to get to the main land of Eleuthera.

Another astonishing sight as we journeyed along was a placed considered by many to be the eighth wonder of the world. The Glass Window Bridge located between Upper Bogue and Gregory Town. What makes this point significant is difficult to explain. On one side of the bridge is very dangerous rough waters with huge waves while the other side is very calm and hardly any waves. The rough water is powerful and in relating the story to David and his family they were informed that the bridge can attest to that. The force of the water often causes the bridge to shift. There were occasions when the power of the water had made it unsafe to drive over. They learnt that it was an important link because it joined North Eleuthera to Central and South Eleuthera.

"What a view", expressed David. He was captivated by the water and the high rock formation.

Susan became somewhat timid because she saw it as a menace, there was only room for one lane of traffic and the driver had to be on the look out to see if any traffic was coming from the opposite direction. To David and his family it was a relief when they were on the other side of the bridge and began to experience the sights of many gentle rolling hills.

They soon passed through Gregory Town, a picturesque settlement clustered around a small, semi circular cove where the best pineapples once grew and were once shipped all over the world. James pointed out the red soil which is believed to be the main ingredient that allowed the pineapples to grow and give it such a good taste. He also told them about the annual Pineapple Fest and that there was dancing and a pineapple eating contest. It occurs the beginning of June and he encouraged them to visit the following year. What also was interesting to them was the information they got from another passenger who shared that they were many rental homes along the shore line. These, they were told, were actual homes of winter residents and they allowed agents to rent them out during special times of the year. From what was said, this type of living was popular because there were only a small number of hotels on the island.

It was such a long drive and David, Laurel and Susan were delighted with the conversation and the new knowledge that they were now privilege to. Susan did not remember seeing any schools along the way and questioned James about that. They learnt that the settlements were spread out towards the interior of the island and what they were seeing was just the front portion. In that regard, schools would be more in the centre of the settlement. Fruits and sometimes fish stalls were very popular on the front side.

Noticing a tall round hollow cement structure, Susan wanted to find out what was the purpose. They no longer seemed to be in use because tall trees were growing out of the top of them. Mr. Johnson a senior citizen shared this aspect of the history of the island. He previously lived in Hatchet Bay and was familiar with those old ivy-covered structures which he called 'silos'. They used to store grain to feed the cows in the 1960's. From what David and his family gathered Hatchet Bay was once a thriving dairy farm community established in 1936 by Austin Levy. They made ice cream, milk and raised chickens for consumption for the entire Bahamas. Mr. Johnson mentioned how it was so unfortunate that such a good business was not sustained.

Between Hatchet Bay and James Cistern, Mr. Johnson pointed out Hatchet Bay Caves which was described as one of the largest system of caves in the Caribbean. These caves were hidden in the side open space between the two settlements and give the appearance of a vault cathedral . . . and he told them how they believed those caves were shelter for hiding pirates and buccaneers of the Caribbean in their day.

In passing James Cistern, Brian who was quietly relaxing in the corner, came alive and joined the conversation. He shared with David and Laurel about the Saturday event. Every week end residents of James Cistern hold a Bahamian style cookout, where you can purchase native food such as fried fish, peas and rice, macaroni and cheese, pineapple tart, coconut tart and potato bread. Of course both David and Laurel were not familiar with potato bread and almost in unison asked 'what was that'. Brian, who was a local young man and was good in the kitchen, had no difficulty explaining how it was made from sweet potato and other ingredients. It sounded good to them and they promised to try it. David and Laurel listen with amazement and they too felt that this inconvenience was a lesson to all of them as they listened to the various tales being shared among the passengers.

They had already spent a year on Eleuthera but fail to visit the North and Central part, therefore this journey was a treat for them and they were thoroughly enjoying it. They both remarked how the friendly attitude of the people was prevalent and found their fellow passengers just as charming and attentive.

Entering Governor's Harbour, the capital of Eleuthera, was a blessing because Susan was tired of the long drive and wanted to get out of the bus. At one point she asked her mother to get her something to drink. Mr. Johnson heard her comment and encouraged the bus driver to stop at the food store. David, Laurel and Susan were all happy to get out and walk briefly in the township. Susan ran off to get her drink. David commented on the formality regarding how the other passengers addressed each other as: Mr. or Mrs—followed by their surname—this was unusual for them because for most part everyone in the UK used first name. When this was raised with Mr. Johnson he explained that it was a cultural thing. He even told them that 'auntie and cousin' were also labels widely used when referring to some persons who don't necessary have to be related.

Looking across from where they stopped for the drink, David admired what he later learnt was picturesque Cupid's Cay jutting out towards the sea. The remains of the clapboard house that housed the first US Embassy in The Bahamas supposed to be still visible. It also has a small resort called Harbour Inn. Continuing the journey to Rock Sound along the shore road, St Patrick's Anglican Church was pointed out to them and the dock where the fast ferry docks on its arrival from Nassau. Laurel made a mental note to return and explore Governor's Harbour and some of the other settlements at a later date.

The remainder of the journey was uneventful and everyone seems to be anxious to get to their respective homes. Once at Rock Sound Airport, taxis and relatives were waiting for them and to the delight of David, Laurel and Susan, Bahamasair had arrived and their missing bag was delivered while they were making the journey from North Eleuthera. This was excellent because it saved them from making another trip to the airport. They were happy that Pineapple Airline was able to get their bags on Bahamasair.

Chapter 12

ery quickly they were on their way to Cape Eleuthera, passing through Deep Creek which they now refer to as their first love. Arriving at their home Susan was happy to be able to move freely after those hours driving from the North. Not only was she happy to be home but wanted to immediately contact her friends George and Janae. Her father was lenient that night and allowed her to say hello via the telephone and she promised them she would see them the following day. Susan wanted to show off her new school supplies and also to give them the small token which she brought for them from the UK.

They were all exhausted from the trip and went to bed early only to be awakened during the night when the heat in the room became unbearable. A power cut! The light from the moon allowed Laurel to move about and locate the flash light prior to opening the windows and a sliding door. No sooner did she open the sliding door, she got an outburst from Susan who already was upset about the outage and with the door open that heightened her sense of insecurity. David rushed to comfort her and to assure her that it was safe to have the door open. In the

UK they rarely had power outage; therefore this was new to all of them despite the fact that they experienced this situation earlier in their relocation. Fortunately it did not last long and they remembered their real estate agent telling them from time to time it would happen. This was confirmed during a conversation they had with James who was one of the managers at the power station while driving from the North.

After the episode with the lights and falling back to sleep, they all got up early and looked forward to the day. Laurel decided to unpack, Susan waited for her friends and David planned to drive into Rock Sound to get some groceries and fresh fish.

Was that a knock on the door thought Laurel and where is Susan because she was at the front waiting for her friends. Approaching the door there was Nina and Rachel looking concern.

"Laurel they both seem to have shouted together, there has been an accident and we came looking for David" said Nina.

"Accident?" said Laurel. "Not my Susan. Where is she?"

Nina and Rachel immediately saw that they had caused her grief and quickly cleared up the matter. Susan was fine but they wanted David to assist with rescuing a child who had drifted out to sea on a beach inflatable ring.

What a relief to Laurel although she realize she was being selfish. David had long left for Rock Sound and she quickly followed the ladies on to the beach area where families were celebrating the last of the summer vacation. The child in question was ten years old and for a brief minute no one paid attention to her but later hear faint cries and on looking out to the water they saw her already a long distance from the beach. Bobbie from the Cape School heard the screams of the family and he mobilized two speed boats while Nina and her friend drove to get David.

It was a close call for the child because she had drifted about ten miles out to sea and it was good that she kept hanging on to the tube. The whole community on the beach cheered when they saw her returning on one of the boats. Her mother who was extremely upset shed tears of joy.

Laurel was so caught up with this event that she completely forgot her daughter who was still in the settlement with Janae and George. They heard the news however and got a ride to the beach. She was happy that they did that as she could stay longer with the family and other members of the community. While sitting with them and awaiting the nurse to examine the child, Laurel thought it would be a good idea to have the family over to her home with one or two other persons including Nina and Rachel who thought enough of her family to inform them of the plight.

With the extension of the invitation it was decided that it would take place next Saturday and hopefully with David's approval. She prepared to walk back to her home but not before checking with the nurse who confirmed that apart from being scared the young girl was fine. An immediate prayer of thanks giving was said by Rev'd Toppin who happen to be in the area when the child was adrift.

That was enough excitement for Susan and she willingly went home with her mum and to let it all sink in regarding the details of the events. She found it hard to understand how come her mother was not looking at her knowing very well how attentive her parents are with her. Sometimes she thinks they are too protective especially now that she is almost fourteen.

David who enjoyed his morning in Rock Sound met them on the porch because he had heard while driving back that there was a problem. Giving him all of the details, Laurel and Susan soon began to unpack the items he brought and to prepare for lunch. Laurel mention to David the invitation that she extended to the family before he went for his swim. She did not want him to hear it from other people. He felt it was a great gesture and while going for his swim he began to think about a menu for the occasion.

With all of the grocery items unpacked and putting up the clothing from the trip the family was able to relax and discuss their visit to the UK and the short stop in Miami. Miami in particular was very new to them and they felt that it would be worth returning in the future.

Susan was excited about her return to school and already tried on her new uniforms and books were placed in the new book bag. She told her parents how happy Janae and George were pleased with the souvenirs she brought for them from the UK especially Janae. She specifically liked the school items which had famous sights of London on them. With a new school year beginning and the excitement of continuing her scuba diving, what else will be in store for Susan?

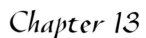
Chapter 13

K eeping her word and also a firm believer of giving God thanks, Laurel made preparation for her small party for the family and some friends of the ten year old who went through that horrible ordeal at sea. Every person in the community knew about the gathering. Susan came home and told her mom that some of the children were talking about the party.

It was Saturday afternoon and one week end before school opened, Laurel included a treat for the children as well. She made some English scones which they would serve with gooseberry jam and clotted cream. In addition there would be coronation chicken, vegetable salad and fruit. She did not leave out her precious bread and butter pudding and hope that it be a 'hit with her guest. There were a few bottles of elderflower sparkling drink which were for those adults who were non-alcoholics. Since learning how to make the Bahamian lemonade, a few bottles were made for the children. Everything was ready and the guests arrived with Nina who was now very familiar with Laurel and her family, brought a guava duff much to Laurel's delight. She only had it on one occasion but found it to be tasty. Rachel and the remaining crowd all assembled some in the living room and other on the porch. David was busy helping the men with drinks and Susan entertaining her friends with her latest gadgets.

What a noise! Everyone seems to be talking at one time about the ordeal and other old stories which were good for David and Laurel. They were still getting used to certain actions and behaviours that were not part of their culture. Joining in the story sharing, David told them about their visit to Bahama House in London and how the Bahamas High Commissioner spoke about the Island and influenced their decision to relocate. After their visit David told the group that he researched the internet to find out more about the Commissioner and was surprise that his job covered a number of countries in Europe including Belgium. From the website of Bahama House he further shared some of his activities including an invitation to the Isle of Wight where he met the Chief Councillor Arthur and Doreen Taylor. This is the largest island of England and located in the English Channel. David continued to share with them especially to let them know that the Isle of Wight had a connection with The Bahamas. The first Bahamas Defence force boats were built on that island. Additionally, the same Lord Mountbatten that got his homemade bread from Mr. Sands in Savannah Sound was the Governor General of the Isle of Wight 1969—1974. Everyone in the room was in awe and was even more excited when David mentioned that from the London Times, a leading newspaper during 2008 Angelic McKay, a Cultural Officer from the Ministry of Youth and Culture together with Barabbas and the Tribe Junkanoo group also visited the Isle of Wight. They conducted cultural workshops with the school children sharing with them skills to construct junkanoo costumes. The work shop ended with a parade where children and adults showed off their creations.

James came by to bring some vegetables from his father's farm in Tarpum Bay was laughing and audible agreeing with David's story. To the surprise of those present, James told them that the High Commissioner was on the parade and that he had seen the costume and the head piece that the Commissioner wore on the Parade. This was a surprise to those present but word soon got around the room that he was the son-in-law of the High Commissioner and visited England in 2009.

Serving the food was not a problem. Laurel had plenty help especially Nina who really had a skill full approach when dealing with such matters. Everyone was able to get what they wanted including a drink and most of all the dessert. Trying the bread and butter pudding was very popular despite the fact that guava duff a native dessert was available. Laurel did not mined some of that being left over because she came to like it and was hoping that some be left over for her to eat at her leisure.

It was Laurel's turn to share and she used a conversation she had with the spouse of the High Commissioner, whom she mentioned was involved with two groups in the UK and found them to be very special. The group waited with much anticipation to see what she was up to knowing that prior to travelling to the UK she worked as the Director of the Probation Department. Laurel assured them that she made her mark by being involved with the Commonwealth Country League Fair Committee. For two consecutive years she was a co-ordinator of the fair programme and co-deputy chair woman of the fair. Laurel conveyed that what she heard Her Excellence enjoyed her role and felt that she made a meaningful contribution because the funds raised were for scholarships awarded to less fortunate girls in Commonwealth Countries requiring assistance for their education. Additionally, she had the opportunity to write an article on Junkanoo and Bahamian food for their quarterly newsletter. Before finishing her sharing Laurel mentioned the another group called 'Connect with the London'. This was spearheaded by the wife of a Conservative MP and specifically put together for spouses of High Commissioners so that they could be shown various places of interest in London. These included a walk in the city to see hidden gardens, art galleries, and museums, the Old Bailey Court, book launches and many other places and events of interest. Nina, the retired teacher was thrilled and commented that the experience was an educational one and felt certain that the knowledge gained would be beneficial to The Bahamas whenever the couple returned home.

"What a wonderful afternoon", exclaimed Rachel to Laurel and David. "My husband and I can't thank you enough for what you have done. The exchange of information has been an experience where you were able to get from us and we were able to hear from you. I am sure the rest of those present also join me in thanking you for your hospitality and one day soon we will return the favour".

The men that assisted and were from the Cape School also boasted how fantastic it was for David and Laurel to put on such an event. They only recently came among the community but already showing that unity was a true factor and should be continuous in the settlement.

Later in the night, David and Laurel reflected on their gesture and were glad that they were able to do something for the community. This also set the pace for their next adventure which they talk about for the past year but did not do anything about it. They both wanted to be more involved in the community and use their skills to empower those they came in contact with. Of course Laurel would be looking for an opportunity to use her life coaching skills as well as she was a part—time Human Resource Consultant prior to relocating. Her eyes were on the primary school in Deep Creek for coaching possibilities or even the Rock Sound High School—Preston Albury. Usually, it was that age group that required coaching much more than the primary children. She promised to put out some feelers regarding that venture. As for the HR skills, she may just have to wait, seeing that it was not much employment in South Eleuthera.

David was not quite sure how he could be an asset to the community. Mind you, there seemed to be a large number of young men both in Deep Creek and in Rock Sound who seemed to be drifting aimlessly, but he did not want to jump to any concrete conclusions regarding their status. He told Laurel that maybe a talk with key people inclusive of the Administrator and other significant person in the communities would give him a better idea of what he could do to contribute to the further development of the settlements. Both of them mused over their wanting to help and the fact that they are now very comfortable and believed they can make a difference. Judging by the fact that those that they have come to know seem comfortable with them and embraced the cultural differences. With those last thoughts, they both drifted off to sleep being very happy and content.

Chapter 14

*H*ow time flies? Laurel was able to get a voluntary position at Preston Albury High School in Rock Sound using her Life Coaching Skills. Initially she spent a lot of time explaining what her task was but soon it became clear to everyone. Not only was she a help in school but pretty soon persons were knocking on her door at home requesting her services.

The community was used to social workers moving about and giving assistance but Life Coaching! That puzzled many residents. Laurel lost no time in explaining that it was a 'process of helping people to move from where they are now to where they want or need to get to'. She further informed those interested that this type of coaching could be applied to a number of areas in their lives such as the home (parenting) work, finances, social life, love, life spiritual life and health. Once this information got out in the community, parents who felt it was useful requested her help and of course the teachers at the high school welcomed her. At school, the young boys in particular presented behavioural problems and to a lesser extent, some of the young girls. It was an exciting time for Laurel because she truly liked coaching and daily she had a varied experience of what went on in the lives of the children in both Deep Creek and other settlement in the South. She continuously showed them how to discover new things about themselves, design a plan, work on any obstacles and form a partnership to help them bring about the change they required. Most of all she emphasised that 'when an individual has life purpose, they will begin to see meaning and structure in the events of their life'. It is this wonderful realization that helps to bring results from the coaching process.

Word of her success with the teenagers soon spread throughout Eleuthera. Laurel found herself being asked to travel to other settlements.

She decided to start a private practice. This was not planned but Laurel and David felt that the request was worthwhile and they eventually introduced a sliding fee and to their surprise clients, had no difficulty with paying. Additionally it was necessary especially when asked to travel to other settlements, at least the funds was able to buy gas which was expensive on the island.

David never got his plans off the ground due to the demands made on Laurel. It was good because someone had to be home to be with Susan after school. He had no problem with being that person to be the care taker and it was a task he was used too even in the UK. Laurel was the partner that was always in demand due to her line of work. His professional background was in IT and he did that from home but was not particularly interested in doing that in Eleuthera.

His interest in working with young men and their development came from a conversation he had with the High Commissioner who was previously the Commissioner of Police in The Bahamas. From his point, the young men in The Bahamas and no doubt Eleuthera in particular would need guidance so that they could become productive citizens and not join gangs or get into trouble. David marvel at the High Commissioner's own story which revealed that he was orphaned at a young age but that did not stop him from rising above his circumstances and becoming Commissioner of Police for the Bahamas 2000 to 2008.

With this information David knew sooner or later he will make a contribution. Recently he was informed by George that there were some unsavoury behaviour taking place and the possibility of some young men may be smoking marijuana. He did not want to act to quickly but get a feel of what was actually happening without bringing any attention to George and besides he wanted to have a short break from the community especially in view of recent events and Laurel busy schedule.

A week-end to themselves was becoming a rarity and they made a conscious effort to enjoy the Thanks giving week end. Most of the teachers at Susan's school were Americans, so the school gave the students Thursday and Friday off. This allowed them to spend a week end in Governor's Harbour but to Laurel surprise; St Patrick's Anglican Church wanted her to speak to the Anglican Church Women group on parenting. How could she refuse when everyone now associate her with speeches and believe she have the answers to help parents with their children?

It was only for an hour so it did not interfere with their short break and at the same time she felt that she was making a contribution to the Governor's Harbour community. In a sense she too was learning from the various groups as well because getting to know more about the culture gave her a better understanding of what was happening to parenting in The Bahamas. There was some similarity to the UK especially the reporting of parental abuse or any other abuse. However it was not to the extreme.

On arrival in Governor's Harbour they located Tippy's Restaurant and also stayed at his Resort, the Pineapple Fields Hotel. They planned to spend the week—end relaxing and taking in the spectacular view of the ocean, once Laurel completed her talk on the Friday night. They were very pleased with the accommodation with its yellow colouring and lots of flowering plants that help to give the surrounding a cheery atmosphere together with the fresh breeze coming straight off the sea.

Early Saturday morning, Susan was up bright and early wanting to go to the beach. Both parents wanted to unwind and they too join in her enthusiasm and went to the beach before having breakfast and exploring the settlement. On their agenda for that day was a visit to the historic Haynes Library and to go to Cupid's Cay.

David, Laurel and Susan were impressed by the structure of the Haynes Library which was originally established in 1897 and in 1996 refurbish and opened to the public. While browsing inside they were informed that a variety of programmes for children and adults take place at the library. A recent summer programme, they were told, saw some children in the community being exposed to jewellery making by using discarded plastic bags.

The library was a non profit organisation, privately managed and has annual fund raisers along with donations to maintain the structure. Fortunately, for those who use it, there is internet available and a nice supply of books. Both David and Laurel enjoyed the tour and felt that it was truly a positive institution in the community and if all children were like Susan the array of books would be of great interest to them.

Leaving their car under the shady coconut palm trees, the family strolled along the causeway to Cupid's Cay where they walked through some of the narrow street which they were told were the original widths when the Cay was founded and developed. There was the large Methodist Church very near the entrance to the Cay and they marvel at the structure which was damaged some years ago by a hurricane but the hard working community was able to restore it to its glory days.

According to a source in the community, the church was about 170 years old. They believe that St. Patrick's Anglican Church which they saw near the Library was built about the same time. The people of Governor's Harbour treasure both of these Churches and they always embrace any opportunity to show them off to visitors. The walk about was like a history lesson but David especially did not mind because he wanted to know more about this land which he now called his home. They found a large

SHARON FARQUHARSON

dockyard which received shipment of goods from all over the world. Additionally, it is the landing spot for The Bahamas Fast Ferry fleet of boats which ply between the island and Nassau.

Like the Cape, David and his family recognised the warmth of the environment. They were happy to find a small restaurant on Cupid's Cay where they could have a bite and to cool off. A quiet moment was out of the question because the friendly staff soon engaged them in conversation wanting to know more about them. Actually one of the waitresses recognised Laurel from the evening talk at the Church and felt that was an opportunity to ask her a personal question concerning her own family situation. Although Laurel was able to say some things to her, she felt it wasn't the place and invited her to come to the Cape on her day off.

The menu was varied and all three of them soon became very engrossed in making a selection; crack couch with fries was Susan's choice and both David and Laurel tried the grouper with peas and rice. Laurel could not pass up the guava duff and asked that she take it with them. The meal was topped off with good old lemonade much to Susan's delight. They had a leisurely lunch, enjoyed the cool breeze and slowly walk back to their car where they began their journey back to Tippy's to settle around on the lovely beach and even plan to take a dip in the inviting blue sparkling water. Both David and Laurel had their favourite books to read but also realized they had to keep an eye on Susan.

Sunday morning dawned with a bright sunshine and after breakfast they prepared to attend the morning Church service at

St Patrick's. Laurel in particular was looking forward to the visit because she had made some friends with some of the church ladies during the Friday night talk.

The high mass service was wonderful. There were much more servers and they even had a mixed choir which sang beautifully. Yes she did notice some of the ladies from Friday night and at the end of the service, Gay came over and invited the family to have some tea and sweets. There was one sweet in particular that caught their attention, coconut trifle which was made with a pastry with coconut on the top. When Gay was questioned about how it was made, she happily called Janice who spent most of her time making those sweets for her as well as interested persons who may wish to purchase them.

Leaving the church they went back to Tippy's and planned to start their journey back to the Cape after having a buffet lunch. About mid afternoon, they finally left for the drive south. All too soon they were in Palmetto Point and was met by a marching band and a group of men and women marching and wearing uniforms with very nice regalia. Being curious, they parked on the side of the road and watched the event and at the same time tried to get a sense of what was happening. This settlement, like most islands have what is known as the Friendly Society, where people meet. David suspected that it was like a social club where activities took place for those residents who are members. This occasion reminded him of a story shared by the High Commissioner who spoke about his days as the Police Commissioner. He told David that he once had an annual Police

Church Service for the police officers from all of the settlements in Eleuthera and they too marched through the community of Hatchet Bay. It was something that was done annually in Nassau but he tried to bring it to the islands. Laurel and David felt that the march must have been similar and the enthusiasm of the people must also been the same. What a wonderful climax to their weekend.

Chapter 15

S usan could not wait to tell her friends at school about her week—end trip in Governor's Harbour. She was particularly impressed with Cupid's Cay and Tippy's beach. Her friends were delighted to hear her story because they seldom got an opportunity to travel to that part of the island.

They soon, settled down in school and were very active in the class room as well as the many field trips and Susan's specialty, scuba diving. She still struggled to master the techniques required although she tries to follow the instructions of the teacher. Her class—mates also helped her because they naturally are in the water much more than she does because it is a pass time for the islanders. The water temperature is always pleasant although it is not so popular during the winter season. Meanwhile the students were looking forward to their Christmas holiday.

Prior to the holiday the whole school was preparing for the Christmas carolling project. Each Tuesday they met in the dining room to practise Christmas carols which they will sing to the senior citizens in Deep Creek, Wemyss Bight and The Cape.

Parents were asked to donate food items for the bags and each school child would be responsible to take the bags into the home of the senior citizen.

While preparation for this activity was taken place, an even bigger event was taking shape, Junkanoo. Junkanoo is one of the biggest parades in The Bahamas and usually takes place on Boxing Day and New Years day. It is a competition between various groups for the coveted prize of best costume and music. All of the settlements on Eleuthera take part in this competitive event. Deep Creek Middle School would be appearing for the second time and Mr. Fox the Cultural teacher together with the students chose an African theme. Everyday students worked feverishly to complete their costumes and practise their music. It's mostly the music that really helps groups to win in addition to the costume. Susan was one of the dancers and she practised hard to make sure she got her steps right because the route for the parade starts at the Tarpum Bay Primary School and moves very slowly along the Queens Highway which is the main street and end near Carey's gas station. She needed a lot of energy to keep dancing especially since she was not used to the rigorous moves. What was a surprise to her was although it was a Christmas event, for the Family Islands the period for the parade could go into the New Year.

Seeking to know more about Junkanoo, Laurel surf the internet and found out that historically it dated back to the time of slavery when slaves were given three days off at Christmas time. Further details revealed that the slaves wore scary masks and cavorted about freely on the islands to the beat of homemade instruments.

After her practice session at school, during dinner Susan described to her what would be expected of her during the Junkanoo parade. She immediately told them how it reminded her of Carnival in Notting Hill.

"Susan, you remembered Notting Hill Carnival?" said her mum. Laurel found it almost impossible to believe because they took Susan to see that parade when she was six years old. It was an event that occurs annually during the last week end in August and it is a Caribbean parade based mainly on the Carnival parades which take place in Trinidad, Antigua and many other Caribbean islands. Lots of musicians, dancers and DJs take part in colourful elaborate costumes and the sounds of the Caribbean pulsating music along the route. Included in the festivities would be food and drinks all with Caribbean flavour. Susan smiled at her mother and shook her head acknowledging that she remembered some of the details. Sharing the history of the parade with Susan, Laurel told her how it had started at St. Pancras Town Hall in London in January 1959 as a response to the depressing state of race relations at the time.

Meanwhile her Dad was eagerly encouraging mum to open the mail which he brought from the post office. They got news from relatives in London who shared with them the fierceness of the riots. They were aware that they occurred but did not realize the seriousness of what took place. When Laurel heard about a familiar furniture store being destroyed by fire she was near tears. As far as she knew, the Furniture store was around since she was a little girl and she remembers visiting with her parents to select furniture for their home.

"What a shame" she said to David, as he too tried to take in what had happen.

They were not able to get all of the news from their television but now with the information from Laurel's sister they recognised that a lot of damage was done not only in Croydon but in Pecking, Clapham, Liverpool, parts of Manchester and other cities. The UK always prized itself on being peaceful but with pictures being shown all over the world of young people throwing missiles at the police and breaking into stores were disappointing for them. A newspaper clipping included in the mail, helped David and Laurel to realize that although it seemed bad, riots were around in London for years. The clipping revealed that historically from early as 1381, 1780 riots occurred and more recent ones occurred in Brixton during 1981, 1985 and 1995.

"The shooting of the man in Tottenham started it all, said Susan and what do they expect the people to do. That man most likely had many friends".

David looked at Laurel and they both appeared startled to hear their daughter seemingly taking sides. Quickly they took steps to help her to be more objective. They were not really sure themselves about what sparked the riots.

Despite the news from the UK, David and Laurel was not letting it get them down. They just hoped that the authorities assessed the situation and if need be, provide guidance through various community programmes for the young people.

So far they have sentenced a large number of persons to prison or youth centres but they have to ensure that while they are in those respective places meaningful programmes would be available so that future riots will be prevented. Susan who was not very clear on what took place questioned her parents and they tried as best they could to explain but at the same time let her know that that type of behaviour was unacceptable. Her facial expression showed her parents that their explanation was not satisfactory and they felt it was better to hear her views. Wow, they were glad they did. Susan was of the view that the shooting caused the problem and that at home in the UK they treat the 'blacks' badly. David and Laurel were stunned. Is this their little girl? Where did she get such an idea? Trying not to be too rough on her, David allowed her to share her views without recrimination and at the same time tried to get from her where she got the information. George who is a Native American was behind it all and this then became a major concern for this family. They did not mind their daughter interacting with the community but at the same time they need to be more aware of what she was learning from those around her. Spending some time with her and explaining that yes there were incidents of racial problems but from what was revealed in the media and what her Aunt had said, social problems such as unemployment and family relationships inclusive of poor parenting appeared to be the main focus.

David and Laurel noted that incident and promised each other to be more vigilant with Susan and her friends. This was even more important because they were planning to celebrate her birthday with a small party at Sharil's restaurant and the following day they would go into Nassau for a long week end. They were keen to see how it would turn out.

Chapter 16

S urprise birthday party for Susan! "George did you get your invitation for the party and you see it is a surprise. I know how you are with telling everything to your friends", commented Janae.

Not pleased with that remark, George despite their friendship refused to answer and Janae knowing his temperament did not push the issue. Later they both agreed that it would be a fun occasion and was looking forward to it. Every now and then they appreciated a break from the intense studies and additionally they were very good friends with Susan. This would be her fifteenth birthday and why not go all out and have a wonderful time. Besides, they understood her parents would be taking her to Nassau the following day to explore and learn more about the capital city.

'She is lucky and an only child' was heard by Janae and George as they waited with some of the friends who had been invited. Janae and George were together as they usually are and both commented on how well David and Laurel were known in the community. Although the crowd was small, knowing the people in those settlements, some would be mad because they did not get an invitation.

'Shh, shh, she is coming', someone shouted. Of course, the curtains were drawn and the lookout person, Ms. Rachel was doing her best to make sure that Susan was truly surprised.

'Surprise!' was the loud shout when the door open and the lights went on.

'Oh my God' shouted Susan with a gush of tears, as she looked around and she saw her friends cheering. After composing herself chose to go to her best friends Janae and George who both embraced her and had a good laugh. She was really surprised but also happy that her parents decided to have the party for her. Turning to the eastern window she was amazed at the gifts on the table and the home made birthday cake. Everything was delightful. Talking, laughing and greeting other friends and some of the parents soon cause the time to go by quickly. The delicious food prepared by Sharil inclusive of the conch salad was quickly consumed and all too soon the cutting of the cake. This drew lots of speculation because everyone was vying to get the first piece, however Susan was smart and gave both of her parents the first piece of cake. George was very disappointed because he thought that special piece was for him. Not to be out done, George quickly thought that he could get the first dance. The DJ got the music going and knowing that the party would end at eleven George planned his strategy. He first had to build up courage to dance but felt it was something he could do; after all he was almost fifteen and had not danced with other girls before.

"Let's dance Susan", said George. To his surprised she was eager to get on the dance floor. Although she had been on the island for a few years she still did not have the island rhythm for dancing. Nevertheless, George slow danced one number and went right into the next number which was fast. No, she did not get all the steps right but who cared. He was having a ball and very happy that he got to have the first dance. Satisfied with his accomplishment he went on to find Janae while other friends got a chance to dance with Susan.

"Oh look", said Janae, "Susan's parents are dancing too and many other adults as well. Boy this is a good party!"

The dance floor was full and everyone was having a great time much to the delight of Susan who was so grateful to everyone who came and made the occasion a success.

Looking forward to her trip to Nassau, Susan went off to sleep anticipating a wonderful trip.

Chapter 17

*L*eaving Cape Eleuthera the following day for the drive to Governor's Harbour, David, Laurel and Susan spoke eagerly of their journey to Nassau on the Bo Hengy fast ferry. They spoke about this being their first trip but looked forward to many more trips because they wanted to get to know Nassau and Susan even hinted that she may want to attend the College of The Bahamas. Both David and Laurel were surprised because they thought she wanted to return to England.

On arriving in Governor's Harbour, just outside of Cupid's Cay they stopped at Sunset Restaurant and got a quick meal before going on to the dock to wait for the ferry. They meet Jay and her husband on their previous trip to Governor's Harbour and was pleased with their food.

Once they were finished with their meal, they continued the drive to the dock. They were just in time to see their ferry docking as they drove up. After parking the car, David joined Laurel and Susan in the line as they waited to board. Each of them carrying their overnight bag soon marched up the gang plank and entered the ferry.

'Wow' exclaimed Susan. She was surprised at the interior of the ferry and quickly moved to a table where she could sit and watch television. David too, marvelled at the atmosphere because he had conjured up in his mind that they would be in a stuffy boat for the next two and half hours. He told Laurel that everything was beyond his expectations. Meanwhile they settled themselves and enjoyed the ride and only had the ocean and distant cays to look at as they made the trip to Nassau. Few passengers were down stairs and one in particular was engaged in conversation with Laurel. Apparently they met previously because David knew she was community minded and especially since she had been speaking at various churches and schools. Additionally she has her private practise with young people. Both of them were busy sharing child rearing stories despite the fact that there were cultural differences. David heard them discussing child abuse and noted that the UK's strategy for dealing with it was similar to what was happening in The Bahamas. Children from both countries seemed to have the upper hand and report parents and teachers if they felt they were aggrieved. The other passengers clearly indicated their displeasure and hoped that the government would seek to change the policy.

Meanwhile Susan had taken a nap and now was wide awake. The lights of Nassau were very visible thus indicating that they were almost at Potters Cay Dock. Their driver for the few days was Mitchell and they were told to look for a tall dark skin man with a sign with their names. Gazing through the glass windows, slowly the ferry came into the dock where a crowd of people gathered which was similar to when boats arrived in Eleuthera.

'That ride was good Daddy and I am now looking forward to seeing what Nassau is like. Janae told me so much about it and so many places to visit; we may not have the time'.

David could see that Susan was bubbling over with excitement and anxious to leave the dock but they had to get their bags and then it was the matter of finding the Driver.

"David, I am Mitchell, your driver for the next few days".

"Hi there, glad to meet you and let me introduce you to my family; Laurel, my wife and daughter Susan. These are all of our bags and we are ready when you are".

Mitchell escorted them to his taxi and they slowly weaved themselves along the narrow and congested stripe of road and moved towards the main road which Mitchell told them was East Bay Street. Prior to that he told them a bit about Potter's Cay which not only is it a dock for boats but a place of entertainment, and a fish and vegetable market. Most of the vendors had left because it was late when they arrived in Nassau. However, there were a few men playing dominoes and in the distance there was some music.

Already, David and his family observed that the environment was different from the quiet settlement of Cape Eleuthera. This for them was a taste of things to come. They were open to new experiences and from all indications their driver seemed to be the right person to show them around and share information on the island. While driving to their hotel he shared with David and Laurel that their hotel was previously the site of Fort Nassau, one of the forts that help to protect Nassau from pirates. Additionally, this same site had a well from which Blackbeard, a leading pirate in those days watered his ship and a former Governor; Woodes Rodgers hung a dozen pirates. With this type of information David told Laurel and Susan they would be staying in a historical hotel.

Their arrival at the Hilton Hotel was smooth, and with the assistance of Mitchell, they were checked in and safely in their room which overlooked the harbour. Plans were finalized for them to be collected after breakfast the following day. Being exhausted from the ferry trip Susan was soon fast asleep in the adjourning room. David and Laurel poured over various brochures and selected activities for their trip prior to going to bed.

While waiting for the driver they got their first glimpse of Nassau in the day light and saw that they were on the beach and that the hotel was in the down town area. Nearby was the famous Straw Market which they planned to visit once they returned from their morning drive.

"There is a lot to do", said Susan and she told her parents "that she wanted to visit Pirates of Nassau because George told her that it was fantastic".

Being engross with the view they did not see their driver arrive.

"Hi there, are you ready for your morning tour?" said the driver.

Of course the family was ready and eager to begin exploring the Island that they heard so much about. The High Commissioner shared so many details with them of places to see and things to do.

Mitchell told them that since he had started telling them about the former Fort Nassau, he would take them to see Fort Charlotte, which was a short distance from the hotel. Moving along West Bay Street, they passed Long Wharf which is a nearby beach to the hotel and is used by many tourists who came off the cruise ships. They saw colourful booths with coconuts and other fruit drinks, a small number of other vendors inclusive of hair braiders and those peddling small souvenirs. David and his family admired the blue waters gently rolling onto the shore and the number of tourist who must have gotten an early start. Shortly thereafter, they arrived at Fort Charlotte and they were able to get out of the car and take in the view of the harbour. They watched the cruise ship leaving the Island being cleverly guided by two tug boats. They were informed by Mitchell that on some days there could be as many as five or six cruise ships at the Prince George Dock which is an amazing sight.

Bringing their thoughts back to the fort, the driver walked with them towards the structure and shared it significance. He told them that there were historical links as well in that it was built in 1794 under the governorship of Lord Dunmore and also for the use of defending the island. Present day history is inclusive of the fact that it was the site of The Bahamas Independence celebration in 1973 and the park itself is now known as Clifford Park. Both David and Laurel were keen to hear more because they were aware that the High Commissioner mentioned this park and the fact that while he was Commissioner of Police he had many occasions to be in attendance at ceremonies at this venue. This was confirmed by the driver who also knew the High Commissioner in his present role as well as when he was the Commissioner of Police. He further explained to them that the Fort is a tourist attraction, administered by a section of the Ministry of Tourism. With Tourism development the Fort was used for a number of activities and was intermittently commercialised and periodically spruced up to make it pleasing to the eye.

In the distance, the Driver pointed out The Bahamas Cricket Club. 'The quintessential English summer game . . . followed the Union Jack to every corner of the Empire including The Bahamas'. David was very interested in cricket; being familiar with that game because in the UK he always attended games at the Lords Cricket Ground. He told Mitchell of many exciting games between England and the West Indies Cricket Teams or Teams from India and Pakistan. He heard however that the game '. . . had a less profound and lasting effect on The Bahamas'. In 'Nassau, cricket has since wilted through competition from many other activities, and is kept alive only by a handful of enthusiasts, most of them not Bahamian—born'.

Mitchell told them that there was a restaurant at the club and that the proprietor who is an English man with a Bahamian wife prepared a mixture of Bahamian and UK meals. This interested both David and Laurel and they promised to go there before returning to Eleuthera since it was in walking distance from their hotel.

Continuing their journey, their Driver took them to the famous fish fry, Arawak Cay.

'What an array of cafes' said Laurel as she was travelling along the narrow road. 'Do they make any sales Mitchell? There seem to be so many of them'.

Mitchell assured them from what he understood each of the vendors do very well but it also depends on the activities taking place. He pointed out the green space and indicated to them that many fund raisers take place which could be concerts or cook-outs.

"Cook-out!" echoed Susan

The driver told Susan that cook-outs occurs when groups wanted to raise funds either to help with medical expenses, health runs, charities or just individuals trying to make some extra money.

Seemingly satisfied, Susan continued admiring the number of vendors.

Pointing to the new development on Arawak Cay, Mitchell explained how the area would eventually become the shipping port and that this was important so that Bay Street, the centre of the town would not have to have large containers and other shipping items being moved through the town which is already congested with traffic.

Leaving the area, Mitchell continued west to Prospect Ridge where he was able to point out to the family some areas of the new development by Bah-Mar a Chinese based Construction Company. They are responsible for the regeneration of the western district inclusive of building new hotels. Although residents are unhappy with the diversion, the end result is looking really good. It has taken a long time he told them, but now that it has started, many persons are being employed.

David reminded him that he needed to fit in a visit to Paradise Island so they can see and possibly spend some time there. With that the family realized that there was so much they wanted to see but Laurel reminded David that there will be many more trips to Nassau but for now they wanted to get back to the hotel, relax and also go to Bay Street. With that plan they returned to the hotel and looked forward to the late evening outing.

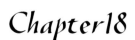

Chapter 18

*B*eing prodded by Susan to continue exploring Bay Street and the surrounding area her parents left the hotel and they finally found the Pirates of Nassau Museum, much to her delight. She could tell George and Janae that she visited and confirm the excitement that they told her about. For Susan, learning about the pirates was new to her because the little bit of history that she learnt prior to leaving the UK didn't go into any detail. That experience revealed that piracy in The Bahamas lasted for thirty years and it was said that Nassau attracted the greatest concentration of pirates seen in the new world. Her parents were just as excited and spent their time also looking at the piratical merchandise, picking up some items for friends back in the UK. Among themselves David, Laurel and Susan marvel at their experience and continued their walk but not before going into the Cathedral which was very near the museum.

Laurel of cause heard David's negative comment. He did not want to visit the Cathedral, but she simply led the way and on entering the building they were both amazed at the interior, particularly the shiny clean tiles on the floor. Otherwise, it resembled the typical cathedrals they were used to seeing in the UK only on a smaller scale and with the usual plaques of departed loves ones on the walls and stain glass windows.

The Sexton or care taker of the church shared with them that Christ Church Cathedral was situated on that site since 1723 and that the establishment of the Anglican bishopric of The Bahamas was in 1861. They were further informed that it followed the parochial pattern of the established Church in England... Knowing David's limited patience Laurel wasted no time, she exited by the side door and they journeyed toward the Straw Market.

"What's happening here and why are they in this tent and I am hot", complained Susan to her parents.

They too were feeling the heat from the hot weather as well as the fact that the canvas from the tent made it worst. They admired the goods but did not spend much time inside and were happy to see a vendor near the back entrance selling cool drinks. Standing near the vendor they engaged her in conversation regarding the set up and they were given an historical overview of their present conditions. They were told that the tent was temporary due to a fire on September 4th 2001 which destroyed their building. At the same time the vendor was proud to point out their new building which they should move into in the not too distant future. Meanwhile, Susan wanted to know how the market got started and how they were able to make the straw dolls and the other lovely items. With great enthusiasm, the vendor gave a brief historical perspective, telling them that the industry was developed as an adjunct to the Tourism industry in 1920. She indicated how the Family Islands also played a role because they were the ones to provide the raw material, Long Island for example was one of the islands that shipped raw material and weaved the basic plait for the vendors in Nassau. Mind you she indicated that some islands also produced products and noted designers like the late Ivy Simms from Long Island, Judy Rolle from Bimini and Joseph Laroda from Abaco all made their contributions. This Vendor was very knowledgeable. She did not want to leave out any information so before concluding the conversation she told Susan that the bags were further enhanced by the use of shells and raffia, which provided beautiful decorations. Taking up one of the bags from a nearby vendor she pointed out the shells and the raffia.

Susan was very much enthralled with the story and thanked the vendor even before her parents could respond. Being very pleased with their outing, they decided to return to the hotel and to enjoy its ambience before they are collected to go to Paradise Island.

Chapter 19

*B*etween the Long Wharf beach and the beach immediately behind the hotel, Susan had a wonderful time trying out her snorkelling skills and swimming with the other guests. There were some young people also visiting and they had a ball. David and Laurel marvel at how happy she was despite the fact that it was her first time meeting her new friends. They also reflected on those times in the UK when she would be so sad which sometime led them to think she might be depressed but they were always fortunate that she got over it.

Her happiness was soon brought to an end due to the time they were to leave for Paradise Island. Oh this created an attitude because she was not ready to leave the beach.

"Do I have to go" was her shrilled cry to her mother.

Of course David and Laurel were not leaving her on her own and sternly insisted that she get out of the water and make preparation for the next outing She was not a happy camper but Laurel who is the sterner parent quietly said to David that she would get over it. David who has a soft heart always want to takes Susan side but thanks to Laurel she keeps him on track so that he could recognise that he is the parent and Susan is the child. David knows very well that Laurel would lecturer him on the virtues of good parenting and that some of what is happening with young people is the result of parents becoming friends with their children instead of parenting them into productive adults.

By the time they were ready to leave Susan was back to her old self and was dressed and waiting anxiously to go down stairs. Laurel winked at David so he too could note the changed behaviour.

'David we need to hurry because the High Commissioner has arranged for us to have a drink with his sons before leaving for Paradise Island', said Laurel.

'Gee, I forgot that, anyway I am almost dressed. Do you want to go down stairs just in case they are early?' replied David.

Laurel had no problem with that suggestion because Susan and herself were already dressed and simply hanging around. Off they went and sure enough the two young men were waiting for them in the foyer. She immediately identified them because the younger of the two looked exactly like their father.

After getting their drinks and meeting Susan, David joined them and said how happy he was to meet them. Both of them spoke of their careers and they seem to be quite happy working for their respective insurance companies. The older son was a manager and enjoyed his role. Additionally he spoke about his various ventures because he was determined to be a business man and is currently working on a project that he hopes will propel him into the business world. David commended them for their commitment to their jobs and encouraged them to continue and to perform to the best of their ability.

The elder son knowing that they were on their way to Paradise Island thanked David and Laurel for seeing them wished them safe passage on their return journey to Eleuthera. Not to be out done, the youngest son invited them to 'Danny under the bridge' if they had the time. This was a stall on Potter Cay dock serving native food.

With that visit behind them, David and his family wandered to the front door to see if Mitchell had arrived. Sure enough he was on time waiting patiently for them to appear. Once settled in the car they were on their way along Bay Street to the bridge to make the journey over to Paradise Island. They went over the newest of the two bridges and returned over the one that was in place very early in the development of the island. Nevertheless, while over there they enjoyed the ambience particularly the large aquarium where a variety of fish was on display. They were fortunate to have supper in the restaurant where the aquarium was located. Susan was overjoyed as she watched the fish swimming in the water together with sharks, stingrays and many other species.

They had a wonderful time during the meal and even engaged the waiter to give them a bit of history on the development of the island. The waiter who was very personable told them how the island is the glittery focus of Bahamian Tourism with the world famous Atlantis mega hotel towering high over the crystal blue waters and that it was built by South African tycoon Sir Sol Kerner. The animated waiter even gave them a bite of history in that Paradise Island went through a period of changes; starting at the very beginning when it was known as Hog Island and not very valuable. It was used to cultivate live stock—wild pigs. David, Laurel and Susan appreciated the short history lesson and really admired the present environment and saw the Island as truly a wonderful treasure of The Bahamas.

Before leaving Paradise Island although it was dark, Mitchell took them on a tour of the island. They were able to see the Cove and the Reef hotels. These were some distance away from the main Atlantis but there were shuttle buses that moved guests throughout the island. What was very noticeable was the number of tourists moving about. They learnt that the hotel usually attracted high end tourists and it would appear from the numbers present they had no problem paying the required charges. Paradise is truly paradise.

Going slowly over the older of the bridges, they heard some of the local music being played under the bridge. They seemed to be having a great time with many native residents enjoying the night.

All too soon they were back at their hotel looking forward to a good night sleep and being ready for their final outing in the morning when they would visit St. Gregory's Church, the home church of the High Commissioner.

"What a wonderful structure", exclaimed Laurel to a sullen David and Susan. They both were not very pleased with her for waking them up so early in the morning to come to early morning church. The family however knew that wherever she goes, once there is a church they will attend. Besides, they particularly asked the High Commissioner about churches and he graciously suggested that if possible visit his church so here they were sitting in a splendid Church with a picture of Jesus in the large stained window overlooking the altar. Arriving just in time, they joined the service. She looked across at David to see if his countenance had changed; he could not be going to communion still being annoyed with her. Of course not! Laurel knew her husband well and was happy that she insisted that they visit this Church before returning to Eleuthera later in the afternoon. This was actually the conclusion of a wonderful trip to Nassau and hopefully will not be the last.

One thing was noted, was that the Church, lasted for almost two hours much longer than they expected. Laurel did not mind the length of time because she always enjoyed attending church services.

After leaving the church, Mitchell made his way to Rudy's restaurant for stew fish before taking them to the hotel. Susan reminded her parents that she wanted to go on the beach one more time before they left for Governor's Harbour.

Breakfast was wonderful. The stew fish was delicious and enjoyed by David and Laurel but of course Susan wanted the usual eggs and bacon. Additionally they all found the Johnny cake to be tasty. Feeling very stuffed they returned to the car and was taken to their hotel. While Laurel was packing their clothing and souvenirs, David was watching Susan in the water and at the same time chatting with Willy, one of the tourists who were also leaving later in the afternoon. They shared their experience and Willy indicated how he would return later in the year. David told him that he lived in Eleuthera. Willy was very interested in that information because he thought David was living in London because of the accent. David told him it was a long story but several years ago he and his wife and daughter relocated to Eleuthera where they are enjoying life to the fullest and leaving behind the stress of the UK. Willy liked that and wanted to hear more about Eleuthera because he said that recently he and his wife was considering leaving New York but did not quite have a destination in mind. David was happy to spend a few moments talking about Eleuthera but encouraged him to surf the web for additional information. Laurel joined them and confirmed that Eleuthera is the place to be and told Willy they would be looking forward to hearing from him once he did his research. David handed him his card and they turned their attention to getting Susan out of the water and completing their final preparation for travel.

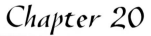

Chapter 20

After saying thanks to Mitchell, David, Laurel and Susan boarded the BoHengy for their journey home. David enjoyed the trip and informed Laurel that they will be passing through Nassau again because their next visit would be Long Island where he hopes to see the birth place of the High Commissioner. Mean while he will be surfing the net to find suitable accommodations and they too have to be mindful of Susan's school attendance, therefore they have to go when she is on school vacation. Laurel had no problem with that she just needed to organise her appointments because she still had a cadre of clients. She loved helping the community, even when she had to travel to other settlements.

After settling on the Bo Hengy and to their surprise, there was a large crowd travelling and from what they gathered there was a school group going up to spend a week exploring Central Eleuthera. Susan was happy because she had grown to be very sociable and very easy to make friends so this was an opportunity for her to make more friends.

Susan already engaged Aura, one of the visiting group members, to tell her more about their trip. Hearing her accent Aura was visibly surprised but Susan quickly told her about the UK and this seem to settle her and she appeared to be more relaxed and informed her that it was an agricultural trip and that they were looking specifically at the growth of pineapples. Susan shared with her how she sometime ago visited such a farm and was intrigued to see how they grow on top of the plant. They were soon joined by Toni who wanted to know about the UK. Susan shared with them her love for the beaches on Eleuthera. When she went to the beach in the UK, which was very seldom due to the weather, it was covered with pebbles and in some cases the water was muddy. Another interesting point shared was the fact that she lived very near the Palace and often walked along the street where it is located.

"No Toni, I never been to the palace but my parents told me that the Queen is very visible. She attends and host many functions where she invites people from around the country." said Susan.

Toni was surprised about that information and continued to listen to Susan who also shared that diplomats were fortunate. They had the opportunity to see the Queen during Commonwealth Day, the Garden parties and in November when she hosts the Christmas party.

David was listening to his daughter converse with her peers and was proud that she answered maturely and seemingly satisfied those around her.

In the distance were the lights of Governor's Harbour and it was time for them to prepare to disembark and for the long drive to Cape Eleuthera. Susan already exhausted mentioned how she was ready for her bed and there would be no doubt that she would sleep on the way. Nevertheless David and Laurel would have the opportunity to reflect on their trip and most likely begin to plan the next visit.

Unexpectantly, the next visit to Nassau for David occurred about a month later. He had to travel to the UK urgently to complete the long awaited sale of their home which was located in the affluent area of Mayfair. Although Laurel wanted to travel with him being the stronger partner she allowed him to go but not before she gave him instructions regarding the closing price on the house and it was final. Susan was preparing for The Bahamas Junior Certificate (BJC) examinations and there was also some talk about her going as an exchange student with a family in the US. They were not sure about that, being the protective parents that they were but nevertheless they informed the school that they would give it some thought.

David meanwhile arrived safely and hoped to conclude the sale within two weeks. Their agent had done a great job and it was only his signature that was noted on the final papers. This of course gave him an opportunity to have some leisure time on his hand and he visited an exhibition put on by Blue Curry, a native of Spanish Wells and several other UK artists at the Sumarria Lunn Gallery in Mayfair. To his surprise he met the High Commissioner who was in attendance and they had an opportunity to talk about his relocation to The Bahamas. It was a wonderful place to meet. Blue was very pleased to have both of them there and to explain the thinking behind the four pieces he had on display. There was the car tire covered with black and white beans, a coat hanger with parrot feathers, a half covered tire with the same beans and a steel diving spear with floppy disks. The Exhibition was entitled 'Modern Frustrations' and from the work put into making the items both the High Commissioner and David agreed that it must have been frustrating. Imagine trying to fit beans on a tyre and to have a snake skin pattern!!! David always had an eye for high cost stared at the prices, but he later reconciled that artist have to make money too and they spend an awful lot of time shaping their exhibits.

With only a few days left he visited Brighton and caught up with his old friends purchased some chocolates for Susan and Laurel wanted her honey liquid soap from Harrods. The final day at the lawyer's office went well and the money for the sale was placed in his UK accounts. His last night was spent at the theatre watching Billy Elliot, a musical about a young boy who wanted to dance ballet.

Not missing his home at all, David prepared for his return flight to The Bahamas but something caught his attention on the television. Ash! Volcano! What, it might be stopping the flights leaving Heathrow Airport? No, that cannot be true thought David. Laurel is expecting him to be in Nassau later that day. Paying more attention to the headlines, David was discouraged because he would have to stay a little longer in London until they got the all clear. Disappointed, he called Laurel and told her the news and he could hear she too was sad that he had to stay longer. The bright spark came from Susan when she came on the phone. She told him to enjoy himself and since he had more time please purchase some more of her favourite chocolate which she had forgotten to tell him to bring. With that request it helped to lift his spirits and he went immediately out to Sainsbury to get a tin of Celebration Chocolates. With lots of time on his hand he later visited and took a tour of the Palace. This was something that he always wanted to do but never got around to doing it. Every year while the Queen vacations in Scotland, the Palace is open to the public from July to September. Thousands of persons, both tourist and residents of the UK take advantage of the occasion. Once he was informed that they put on display all the gowns she wore when she visited the Commonwealth Countries in addition to the gifts she also received. This year he was not too sure what he was going to see but he did hear that the wedding gown of the new Duchess of Cambridge (Katherine) was being displayed. He did not mind what he saw he just wanted to be active so the time could pass while waiting for the volcanic ash to clear up.

Arriving home later that evening he got a message from his cousin Robert who was trying to find out if he had left for The Bahamas.

"Robert just got your message".

"So you did not leave as anticipated and I am hoping that you could accompany me to Brussels", said Robert. "You remember we have a cousin out there and she is celebrating her fiftieth wedding anniversary and I told her you were visiting. Of cause she said to bring you, what you say about that?"

"Go to Belgium? Robert I am ready to return to The Bahamas but you know what is happening I have no control over it, so why not? When are you going?"

Robert was very happy. He gave David the information and they planned to meet at St. Pancras Train Station to board Euro star, the fast train to Brussels. This arrangement cheered up David and he quickly called Laurel to let her know how he was going to pass the time while waiting for the ash to clear up. While taking to her she told him of another family in Eleuthera who was expecting their son to come home for a break but also was delayed due to the ash cloud.

The trip to Brussels was wonderful and David could not wait to share his experience with Laurel. There was a side trip which he was not aware of but he enjoyed it. They went to Bruges for the day and had a ride on the canal which was a popular activity among the tourist. He learnt that Bruges, located in the Flemish region of Belgium, was referred to as 'the Venice of the North'.

While walking he saw many linen shops and knew that he had to purchase at least one of the beautiful pieces for Laurel and of course the chocolates in Belgium were delicious and Susan would definitely be delighted to have some. All too soon the trip came to an end and they were saying goodbyes to their cousin who he had not seen in so many years. The experience was great especially the fiftieth wedding anniversary gathering. There were people from many parts of Europe who were friendly and interested in his new home in The Bahamas.

Now his attention was focused on his return to his beloved new home—The Bahamas. The last news they had heard revealed that the ash clouds had shifted and that flights should be resuming eminently. That was good news and David could not wait to commence his journey. He told his cousin Robert that he would make inquires and try to get on the first available flight.

To David's surprise, there were a number of seats available and the following morning he was boarding the morning direct flight to Nassau, looking forward to getting back to the warm climate. Those thoughts caused him to ponder about his current home, something that he never even dreamt about but now it is truly a reality. The house in Essex in the UK would now be for vacations.

Chapter 21

*H*ow wonderful to be in Nassau and it would be even better when he finally arrives in Eleuthera. David was very anxious to see his family after the trip to the UK which was extended as a result of the volcanic ash. He made contact with Laurel and Susan while waiting for Pineapple Air. He could hear concern in her voice. Was there something wrong? Not dwelling on that for any length of time David soon became engaged in conversation with James who had visited Nassau for the day. He was able to bring him up to date on hurricane Irene that had passed through The Bahamas while he was in England.

"Hurricane Irene, Laurel did not tell me about that. Was there any damage and did you know if my family was okay?" said David.

James was amazed that he was not aware but quickly hastened to add that Eleuthera did not receive much damage but islands like Cat Island, Acklins and Crooked Island received extensive damage. He further told him that the electricity supply was disrupted but was soon restored and lots of trees were uprooted otherwise he felt the island had survived without any major damage. What a relief. After hearing this, David was more anxious to get home and thank goodness he did not have long to wait. Pineapple Air announced the flight and they were soon airborne for the twenty minute flight to Rock Sound.

Laurel and Susan were at the airport to meet him and greeted him. He was really concerned about the hurricane and asked how they coped with it.

"It was scary" said Susan. While David, Laurel and Susan were aware of hurricanes it was scary actually experiencing it, especially with David being away. Susan's friends told her how they occur almost every year. Listening to them she learnt that hurricanes or tropical cyclone as they are called in this part of the world 'is a storm system characterized by a low pressure centre and numerous thunder storms that produces strong winds and heavy rains, . . . high waves and damaging storm surges as well as spawning tornadoes. "I don't want to go through that again".

Laurel experienced the same emotion but didn't want to acknowledge it in Susan's presence, so she told David they would talk about it later, for now she was happy to have him home safe and sound.

Meanwhile Laurel remembered the note that she received from Susan's School relating to boarding school. It was something that they were aware of when they enrolled her in the school but at the time, it seemed so far off they really did not give any thought to it. Now three years later, a decision must be made and she must find time to discuss it with David. Additionally, since David was away she had an opportunity to observe Susan and her relationship with George and it appeared to her that their young lady was developing a closer relationship with him. She cannot wait to get David to herself there is so much to tell him.

"Laurel you are very quiet, I thought you would have a lot to say to me. Susan have you been giving your mother trouble?" said David.

Forgetting how alert David was Laurel regretted that she did not keep up her usual chatter because what she had to say must be in private.

"David, of course I have a lot to say but thought you would start by telling us about your trip especially visiting your long lost cousin in Brussels".

Wow, that did the trick David readily shared his experience while in the UK and in Brussels during the drive to their home. He told them how he liked the boat trip on the Canal and that so much history about the city of Bruges was shared with them. Especially for Laurel he mentioned the many linen shops with a variety of designs and that he had brought them some chocolate which Brussels is known to produce.

Meanwhile he noticed how dry the trees looked due to the hurricane while he was away. When he was about to mention the same, Susan told him about how frightened she was because the wind was howling and she never knew it could make such noise. Laurel picked up the story and informed him that they both had a scary time although they knew what to expect. Foolishly they refused to leave the house even after Rachel and Nina warned them that it would not be good to remain in their home, which was very near the sea. Laurel told him how the sea water came over the embankment and seeped into the living room. She was awake all night moving furniture and mopping to dry up the water. By early morning the wind had died down and with that the water receded.

"David it really was an experience and we missed you. I didn't want to tell you about my stupid decision to stay in the home until you arrived here".

Reaching over and touching both his wife and daughter Susan, he conveyed to them that he understood their fear.

On arrival at home and while Susan was enjoying the chocolates, Laurel had an opportunity to speak to David about things that happened while he was away. Boarding school for Laurel was first on the list and she was surprised that David seemed to be so composed when she told him about the note from school. When he responded she realized that he did not have a problem with Susan attending boarding school, his only concern was whether she was going to the UK or to the United States. From information that he had received, it seem that most of the students went to the US. His mood was one of happiness in that his daughter had reached the level in the school to be considered to travel abroad for further education. Some time ago he heard Susan indicate that she wanted to be a social worker and as far as he was concerned completing her high school in the US would put her in good position to enter college or university.

Noticing that Laurel had stopped from talking David questioned her about her feelings.

"David you mean you're willing to let our daughter go to boarding school? I feel she is still immature and need to be with us a little longer".

"Immature! Laurel, Susan has grown. Haven't you notice that she does not even sulk and be withdrawn any more. Besides I think she is interested in George. Have you noticed their relationship recently?"

"About George, that was my other point, to discuss with you but it seems you are aware already and seem to be proud of it".

"Now Laurel, Susan is fifteen and going through the normal process of adolescence and we as her parents should be guiding her not fussing over the situation. There is nothing wrong with what is happening but as the parents we must help her to understand what relationships are about and to prepare her for a future with a partner. Also, if you are truly concerned then you should agree that she go to boarding school, thus giving her space to meet with other young people in a different environment.

Remember, George and Janae have been her close friends ever since she came to Eleuthera. Besides didn't you notice them the night of the surprise birthday party?"

Laurel was glad she spoke with David. At times she needed him to help her to put things into perspective and he sure did on this occasion. It makes a lot of sense and already she knew that allowing Susan to attend boarding school would give her a wider experience both educationally and socially.

Susan interrupted their conversation but it was such that they thought it would be a good time to get her views on boarding school. Much to their surprise she had already worked it out and together with George; Susan had selected a co-educational boarding school to attend in the US.

Still not fully accepting of the independence that she saw developing with Susan, Laurel became angry but quickly controlled herself especially after reflecting on the conversation she had with David.

"So Susan you made this decision without discussing it with us" David asked.

"Dad, you always encouraged me to be independent and you know at school they also told us to be independent thinkers, so I thought I was doing something good. Mind you I know I still need the support of you and mum".

Laurel, we both have to accept that our daughter is truly growing up. What we need to do now is to speak further with the school. They told us some time ago that they usually assist with scholarships so it would be worthwhile following up since Susan has made up her mind that the United States would be the place she would continue her studies.

"You know Laurel, although I am happy that she made the decision to continue her studies in the US, I am ambivalent. Somehow, I thought she would have selected the UK but I guess she has been away from there a long time and now see this part of the world has home. Never mind I agree with you and we should see the school principal for further details. While she is still with us, let's go north and finish exploring that part of Eleuthera".

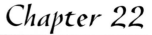
Chapter 22

*T*ravelling North would require planning because there is so much to see in that part of Eleuthera. Laurel confirmed with David and they felt it would be best to do that very early during the summer vacation just before Susan is due to leave for the US. Mean while they did keep the appointment with her present school personnel and obtain the necessary details on the boarding school recommended and they felt that the arrangement was satisfactory. This was especially important to Laurel who was still struggling with the idea regarding Susan leaving home.

The school was well prepared and made most of the arrangement even to the point where they selected a family where Susan can spend week-ends and short holidays. David and Laurel would have an opportunity to meet them when they take Susan to school.

They also learnt that the school is located very near where George was born and had relatives in the area. They would be a family that Susan can go to. Janae would be attending the same school and because the three of them have been together for the last three years, there is no doubt that the transition should be smooth.

With this development taking place David and Laurel finally accepted an invitation to visit George Parents. It was time for the parents to meet again to discuss their children moving together.

They were happy to spend the evening with the family. Rachel and Nina were also present and they reminisced over the time when David and Laurel first came to the community. So much has happened and the highlight of course was seeing these young people now to the age where they will be leaving shortly to go to boarding school. Nina was full of encouraging words for Laurel because she already experienced her daughter leaving home and eventually completing school in the US and found a very lucrative job in the computer industry. She mentioned how she misses her but it also gives her a place to visit on a yearly basis sometimes even twice per year.

David got on well with George's father, Ian who was full of tales about his experience on Eleuthera. He was a keen fisherman and spent a lot of time fishing, sometime having too much fish but the community loved him because of his generosity. When he was not fishing, he spent time among the young men in the settlement. David liked that because for a while he had been contemplating whether to follow up on a comment George had made some time ago concerning the drug use among the young men. He felt better able to handle them now that he heard that Ian was involved. With Susan away at boarding school he would have more time to devote to them especially the days when Laurel was at Preston Albury High School.

The evening ended and both he and Laurel found the event informative and looked forward to many more occasions even if they have to host it. Nina really made Laurel feel more confident about Susan leaving home and for this David was happy because he had no difficulty with it.

With just a week left before Susan was to leave for school David and Laurel began to plan for their trip to the North. They heard so much about Harbour Island and Spanish Wells, they anticipate an exciting visit and with the young people with them, it would certainly be entertaining. The parents of George and Janae willingly gave their consent and Susan was looking forward to the company.

Saturday morning dawned bight and clear with the group eagerly gathering their items for the week long trip to the North. George had never been to that part of Eleuthera so he was just as excited as Susan and her family. Driving would not be difficult because it was one straight road but David was cautious to drive carefully due to the curves in the road. With the radio playing and they half way listening to Junkanoo talks, the group made steady progress and by noon they were entering into Upper Bogue and nearby Lower Bogue. Janae was very familiar with this side of North Eleuthera because her mother grew up in Upper Bogue and she spent many summers vacationing with her grandmother prior to her death. Janae being the spoke person for the group shared with them how, like other Family Islands and settlements on Eleuthera, a number of prominent persons including Canon Harry Ward were products of this particularly environment. David and Laurel learnt that Canon Ward is also a person concerned about the wellbeing of children. He established Comprehensive Family Ministries, which seeks to enable all persons to find and use their gifts to bring wholeness to every family member. This Ministry has four components all centred on the family. While sharing this information, Janae gleefully mentioned his children TV programme because she is hoping that one day he would involve children from islands like Eleuthera to also appear on the programme rather than allowing it to be Nassau centred.

George never heard of this group and he commented on how it might be too late for them because they will soon be going to boarding school but he was just as enthused as Janae for other children to be included.

Noticing a sign pointing to the settlement called Current, David told the group that he would follow the road and sees where it takes him. He was curious because while meeting with the High Commissioner in London, the Deputy Director of Tourism was present, he told him of his home in Current. Janae wanted to know if it was Current or Current Island. David did not know because he thought it was one place. Shortly thereafter, they drove to the dock where the mail boat comes in and they got a clear view of Current Island, which answered Janae's question. The Sea Link, one of the fast Ferries was also docking and to David it looks like the whole community was out to meet the boat. Janae enlightened them to the fact that the transport via the ferry is one of the ways in which Current gets their supplies from Nassau and there are times when passengers also travel via that route to get to Harbour Island and Spanish Wells.

Leaving Current, they felt that they needed to get to Spanish Wells where they planned to have a meal. On their way to Jeans Bay, passing the winding road which goes into the Bluff, Janae remembered that Canon Ward's wife Juliette Ward came from that settlement. A recent retired primary school teacher she recalled that her mother told her that Canon Ward was a teacher and at one point was the principal of Tarpum Bay Primary School prior to going into the church.

Just before reaching Jeans Bay, Susan pointed out an unpaved road on the right hand side of the car and was interested to know where it leads to. David by that time felt that everyone could do with a break and stopped the car for them to explore the road. A sign in the distance said Preachers Cave. Wow, all of the young people were familiar with that name. This was part of their history lesson at school. They learnt that William Sayles and his shipwrecked Eleutheran Adventures in the 1600s sought accommodation in the Caves. This was confirmed for them because at the entrance of the cave they read the placard 'William Sayle shipwrecked at Devil Backbone found refuge here . . .'

For their information it was very near the Devil's Back bone and ten miles from North Eleuthera Airport.

George shared what tales he heard about the Devil's Back Bone, which is a stripe of rough sea between Spanish Wells and Harbour Island. Historically referred to as the 'infamous Devil's Backbone reef, graveyard of innumerable ships . . .' Even on a calm day and with the boat being close to the shore line, there is turbulence. He recalled his mother telling him a story which she heard from Janice, a long time resident of Harbour Island, who travelled that route many times on a mail boat called the Air Swift. In those days people thought that the boat would capsize but fortunately it never happen. Today the fast ferry Bo Hengy, the Day Break and the Eleuthera Express still travel that route but use wisdom to navigate the treacherous water.

After a short distance they were at Jeans Bay awaiting the ferry for Spanish Wells. The dock was battered by hurricane Irene, giving them limited space but the workmen were busy repairing it.

Laurel at this time told David that she felt tired and was not feeling her usual self. Thinking to himself that the hot and humid weather probably was taken a toll on her he immediately got her a bottle of water once they were on the ferry for the short trip to Spanish Wells, a small town on St. George's Cay off the northwest coast of main land Eleuthera. It is a predominantly white native Bahamian(descendant of the first British Settlers in 1600's and Loyalist in 1700's) living in a neat clean tight knit community.

With that bit of information David suddenly remembered that he had attended a local theatre in Greenwich during his recent trip and saw a play called Othello written by William Shakespeare. It was adapted and directed by Robin Belfield who has Bahamian roots and that Othello, the main character was a Bahamian.

"What made you recall this play, David at a time when we are going into Spanish Wells", said Laurel.

"The key word was Loyalist, that triggered my mind and I realized I was about to entered the settlement where the play had its roots".

David reflected that there was a small excerpt in the leaflet that gave an explanation for 'Conchy Joe' going to great lengths to state that it was a slang and derogatory name given to White Bahamians and that these persons were descend from the Loyalists.

"But dad, how does this fit in with Shakespeare's play?"

"Susan what I got from the brochure, like Shakespeare's Moor(blacks), . . . Conchy Joe is a cultural outsider and this play examined the delicate balance on which racial tensions exist . . . The Director's adaption, not only transported . . . the viewers from the Seventeenth Century Europe to the modern day Bahamas (Caribbean), but he distilled the action right down to the core, an intricate triangle of love, loyalty and jealousy". It was a great play and even the High Commissioner, during our visit to his office commented on years gone by when very few dark skinned persons stayed on Spanish Wells. He remembers in the 60's it was himself, another police officer and the nurse. What was interesting and something that you young people should know about, the High Commissioner was a young policeman on this Cay in 1968 when the last riot occurred. Based on his memory of the incident, an Englishman, the later Peter Lloyd had a hotel and attempted to employ persons of colour to work in the establishment which meant that they would have to be on the Island during the night. This was not acceptable to the residents resulted in the disturbance. The hotel was destroyed. The officer along with his colleague had to get help from another policeman from a neighbouring settlement, Bluff. From our drive you remember how far that was from Jeans Bay. Could you imagine them walking that distance in the night with most likely a single flash light? Nevertheless, they got the help they needed and returned to Spanish Wells and with help from Nassau they were able to capture those concerned. David continues to tell them that much has changed in that the community and they seem to be more tolerant of people of colour these days.

Both Janae and George were enlightened by this information and agreed that more of the young people need to know this type of history.

Hearing some of their conversation, the captain of the ferry was keen to know about them and what brought them to the Settlement. David and Laurel were happy to initially say they were from Cape Eleuthera but laughingly told him that they were originally from London and that they were taking a break to visit his beautiful Cay.

"What an array of pastel coloured houses? The roads were immaculate and everybody seems to have a golf cart", said Laurel as they approached the dock at Spanish Wells. David was delighted to hear her speaking so lively, the discomfort mentioned a while back had dissipated. Disembarking was no problem and they anxiously walked to Abner Pinder Rental office, the first one they notice and got a double golf cart for their exploration around the Cay. They noted the small restaurant on the main street and as they drove to the east of the Cay, they noted a Gazebo. David readily associated it with the one the High Commissioner told him about. He recalled that he stated that it was a spot where fishermen gather to discuss issues of the Cay as well as their fishing trips.

"That's really cool", said Susan She noticed that it was built over the water although at that time the tide was out but felt that it must be great to sit there, especially during early evening.

The group continued their journey and noticed that the Streets were numbered rather than having names. It was unusual because street numbers were associated with streets in the United States. Nevertheless following Fifteenth Street they came to a small restaurant where they eagerly alighted the golf cart and wonder inside, seeking late lunch. The young people were satisfied with conch fritters, a cool drink and ice cream.

David and Laurel wanted something more substantial and in this regard the chef was able make them grouper snacks.

They were able to engage the waiter and found out a lot more about Spanish Wells. The Waiter told them how most of them earned their living from the sea. 'These fishermen have the best reputation in the entire Bahamas for their skill at catching crawfish (spiny lobsters)' . . . Known as the fishing capital of The Bahamas this little island exports more lobster than all the rest of The Bahamas combined. They were informed that it was not touristic like the sister island—Harbour Island—but it played a minor role. Enthusiastically she was happy to say that it was a prosperous settlement as a result of their hard work in the fishing and farming industry.

While on Spanish Wells there were many wooden houses displaying a rainbow of colours. In contrast across the bridge on Russell Island which seem to be a more new and modern community, there were many homes constructed with eight inch blocks but similarly the colours were bight and vibrant. From talking with a young man in the community they found out that Russell Island in the not too distant future will be the home to high end development.

Further sightseeing showed that among the elaborate houses nestle in the foliage was some wooden houses assumingly owned by foreign nationals who generally assist in farming the land on that side of Spanish Wells.

Before leaving Spanish Wells they also found out that the people, unlike other islands, provide their own electricity and as a result they do not have the experience of power outages. Susan liked that very much and commented that they should have that same arrangement in Cape Eleuthera. Both David and Laurel winked at each other because they know how she feels when there is no electricity.

All too soon the tour of Spanish Wells was completed and they return to the ferry dock to make the trip to Harbour Island anticipating the delight of the pink sandy beaches.

Chapter 23

*J*ourneying to the Free Island Dock, they passed Gregory Stuart and his family business. They were previously part owners of the Day Break, a mail boat that provided a service for the communities in that part of Eleuthera. More recently, this family now operates a gas station which is conveniently located, rental of cars and a tree farm. David in particular was looking out for this establishment because from what he gathered from the High Commissioner these persons were very reliable and that he always rented a car from them when he travelled to see his daughter in Rock Sound.

Very soon they passed North Eleuthera Airport where they landed on one of their trips from Nassau, continuing on to the dock to get the ferry to Harbour Island. This is where they anticipated seeing the real pink sand which they heard so much about. Laurel recalled that many tales were told to her about Harbour Island and she was looking forward to actually participating in the community via a tour and spending the week.

Whether you journey from Free Island or from around the point from Spanish Wells, the stunting picturesque view of

Harbour Island would be imprinted forever in your mind. This would be the view that David and his family saw as they came to the break of the hill heading to Free Island Dock.

Harbour Island or 'Briland' as known by its residents is one of the oldest settlements in The Bahamas and once served as The Bahamas first capital. The first settlement was founded over 300 years ago almost 100 years before the United States became a nation. It 'is very popular with Bahamians and foreigners alike. It has a number of guesthouses, cottages and small hotels with comfortable facilities on the island and offers the full range of Bahamian water-sports'.

'Briland' has a rich historical heritage dating well back into the 17th century . . . has many historic houses, conveying the old colonial atmosphere of a bygone age'.

The short boat ride from Free Island Dock which also was undergoing repairs was pleasant. However Susan became a bit nervous because the ferry captain was speeding but this was normal. They had to get back as quickly as possible for the next group. There was competition for sales. This was the same behaviour they noticed upon their arrival at dock. Immediately there were a number of golf cart operators trying to get them to rent a golf cart. Laurel left that arrangement to David while she and the young people collected their bags.

Once David settled on a vendor, he was introduced to Prince Mather, a tour guide for the island as well as the historian. Not wanting to be detained he got his number and promised to give him a call.

Before leaving their home David surfed the net and got the name of Romora Bay Hotel and once they got the directions were on their way. They chatted among themselves and all of them agreed that the reception and the atmosphere at the dock were different. Susan being out spoken wondered aloud if the fact that they were touristic and that they always had high employment may be the reason for the competitive spirit.

"You may be right replied, George. Harbour Island supplies jobs for the whole of Eleuthera. I have heard my dad mention that men from as far as Bannermen Town travel here to find jobs because men on this Island seem to lack interest. On the other hand there is another point of view expressed by our neighbour; that is the men charged high fees for their services, whereas men from Eleuthera charge a reasonable fee".

"George, is that so? I must have a word with your father said David. There could be some truth to it because already we have passed a group of men sitting under that tree back there and it is still early afternoon and they should be at work".

Laurel thought the conversation sparked by Susan about high employment was note worthy and told them that they had four days to observe what happens on the island but for now let's enjoy the scenery. While driving they realized their hotel must be outside of the main township but they were not worried about that but recognised that the same pastel coloured houses they noticed in Spanish Wells was also in Harbour Island.

It was a short ride and they were now soon entering the drive way of Romora Bay located in a serene setting with Bright pink picket wooden fence, a superb view of the sea and sunset. David and Laurel were looking forward to their stay in a bungalow and the French cuisine. It was their understanding that the hotel was owned by a French couple.

They really wanted to stay at Pink Sands, which was the oldest hotel on the island but the cost was out of their reach, especially since they had to get three rooms but believed that their selection will do nicely for them.

Immediately the young people were ready for the beach only to find out that it was about a five minute walk. That was no problem to them. However they had to wait for David because there was no way that he would allow them to venture off by themselves. Laurel felt that she needed a bit of rest especially after feeling tired and not her usual self while at Jeans Bay, besides David was always better at such outings.

Seeing that they only had four days she thought that David should make contact with Prince as soon as possible so that they could make the most of the trip. Tomorrow, however, they planned to do their own exploring keeping in mind information they got from the internet and the High Commissioner. Pink Sands was high on the agenda because they knew that was the oldest hotel on the island and it would be interesting to see it and to determine whether the prices they charged was worth it.

Before she could finalize plans for that visit, Susan was expressing her delight about the beach.

"Wow that was great".

Laurel heard Susan before she got into her room that she shared with Janae. Laurel felt as though she only just stretched out on the sofa when she heard David calling her name. They can't be back already it only seem like a few minutes.

"Well Laurel you missed a great time said David. We walked and wiggled our toes in the pink sand, wadded in the water and got a look at Pink Sands Hotel. We were careful with the water because although I was aware of a strong current which could occur periodically, a local man who was on the beach with his horse also gave us a warning about the current. It was interesting talking to him because he has made riding tourist on his horse as a career. You can see that he was enthusiastic about what he do and from what I can see the tourist enjoy his company".

"Did the children ride the horse, although I do not think Susan would want to do so"?

"Laurel, she was the first to ask if she could ride the horse. Sometimes you know we under estimate our daughter and what she is capable of doing. We need to begin to develop more confidence in her and I believe the challenges that we have seen in the past would lessen. Let us make the effort to be encouragers rather than always drawing on negative aspects of her life".

"David you have a point there, and I would try to remember your suggestion".

Susan appeared in the room and from her expression it seems like they had a good time. Janae and George who also came to the door confirmed this. David together with them enjoyed the swim but to her surprise they were busting to share with her the information they got while on the beach. While buying drinks he engaged in conversation with the bartender who told him about the island being divided into 'Up yonder and down yonder'. Where our hotel was located referred to as Up Yonder and tomorrow going into the township would take us Down Yonder.

"Well David, it means that we are beginning to get a better understanding of this island that was populated similar to Spanish Wells. You remember they said that some of the Loyalists migrated here as well".

True to his word and in response to David's phone call Prince kept his promised to visit them during dinner so that they could get an over view of the island. It was their understanding that with the island being three miles long and three and a half miles wide, they should have more than enough time to cover it.

They found out that Prince was a retired local teacher, the island local historian and the author of the Island's history book and that he was passionate about preserving the history of the island. They enjoyed his company but noted that he talked nonstop about the island with such enthusiasm. The island affectionately called 'Briland' is a thriving tourist resort and provides employment for the community, confirmed what they knew already that it sometimes provide employment for residents from other parts of Eleuthera. David and Laurel instantly recognised that Prince was knowledgeable about his home town and even mentioned that he knew the High Commissioner in London. They then realized that he had close ties to the High Commissioner because he was related to his spouse.

He shared how in days gone by whole families were employed at Pink Sands. He also mentioned that the spouse's grandmother, mother, two aunts and an uncle all worked at that hotel. What was funny to David and Laurel because by this time the young people had left the table, one aunt and the uncle, a part from being a waitress and store room keeper respectfully, at the hotel, also provided entertainment for the guests? On Saturday nights they used to dance with buckets of water on their heads. This skill was perfected during the times when these two persons were required to tote water from a cistern for household use.

Tales have it also that staff at the Pink Sands Hotel sometime experience scary moments. The hotel itself is located in front of the local grave yard and sometime persons pulled cruel tricks on the staff when they left work late at nights. There were stories about people covered with white sheets creating apparition during the night to scare employees especially on occasions when there was a recent burial.

Another aunt who cooked at Pink Sand also loved her god children and spent many hours entertaining them on the beach in her spare time. Seagrapes, thatch berries and coco plum were popular fruits which were collected most of the time when such trips were arranged. According to information given these were wonderful and joyful occasions with lots of laughter.

Like all young people Susan and her friends became impatient while waiting for her parents to complete their conversation with the historian. With George and Janae encouragement they left the hotel and caught a ride to the Vic Hum Club which is a landmark in the community. Entering the club, Susan was surprised; she umm and ahhh at the memorabilia around the room. She was of the view that they were going to a dance club. Janae who had some idea about the club quickly told her some of the history connected to it.

"Susan this club was established fifty years ago by the father of the present manager, Humphrey Jr., nick named 'Hitler' and two of his uncles. The music in those days consisted of a bongo box guitar and maracas".

"Janae I am glad you told me that bit of information because to me it seemed like I had stepped back in time. There were so many posters on the walls and now I can see that they were pictures of past performers'. (Literally every square of wall in the outer bar and lounge was decorated with colour print outs of entertainment and sports figures, including three albums by the popular group of the sixties).

"Susan I agree with your view but I also found out that he uses it as a Museum as well".

Janae was happy that Susan and George had a better prospective on the club and indicated to them that the manager was approaching them.

'Welcome to the Vic Hum 'he said and graciously offered to answer any questions they may have. Recognising that they just arrived on the island, he shared with them with an affable attitude the history of the club and the history of music and sports associated with it.

The group upon entering into the uncovered section which double as a basket ball court and the dance floor confirmed the emphasis on sports. When questioned about dancing because that is what Susan was interested in, sadly she was informed that there was no band that night.

Hearing a noise at the entrance they turned around to see David and Laurel anxiously hurrying towards them. Susan could see from her mother's face that they were in for a scolding.

Chapter 24

pprehensively the group waited. Their host was unaware of their concerns. Susan and her friends knew they were in trouble for leaving the hotel. The manager instead was looking at the new comers as perspective customers. He was in for a surprise because Laurel lost her cool and was truly hysterical as she reached out to her daughter. David was shocked because he never seen his wife in such a state and quickly caught hold to her trying his best to bring some order to the situation.

"Susan, shouted her mother, how can you walk out of the hotel without telling us?"

Rather than allowing Susan to take the full responsibility for the event George spoke up and stated how he instigated the trip to the Vic Hum. By this time David had managed to calm Laurel and the host took them to a sitting area where they could better discuss the problem. He already gathered that these young people left the hotel without the consent of their parents. He did not know that two of them were friends of the couple's daughter.

Susan rushed to her mother and gave her a hug which seem to have contributed to opening the flood gate for her mother. Tears flowed and in between she tried to tell Susan how scared she was thinking that something awful could have happen to them.

Susan looking at Janae and George was a bit shocked because they felt very safe although they were a short distance from the hotel. Janae who was familiar with the Island reassured Susan's mother that they were safe and apologized for leaving in the manner in which they did.

David, who was calm throughout the ordeal, felt that the matter could be dealt with when they returned to the hotel. He was captivated by the nostalgic environment and immediately engaged the host so that he could get a better understanding of the posters on the wall. Some of the information was already shared with Susan and her friends so David got a brief summary but was deeply impressed by the ambience. Not only was it interesting but there were other tourists wandering around, some having a drink and others like Susan was disappointed because there was no music. They would have to return on a Saturday night.

'Hitler', the manger wasted no time in telling them also about Barracks Hills which is just a few yards away from the club. Like Nassau in the early days cricket was played on the island on that hill. History has shown that there was a riot in January 1860 because of cricket. '... A group of white 'Brilanders' had leased a few acres of flat land (not known if this was Barracks Hill) in order to play cricket, but their first (and seemingly only) match was disrupted by the local blacks who regarded the area in question as common land traditionally earmarked for market gardening'. This of course caught David's attention being an avid cricketer but due to the late hour they were not able to view the grounds but promise to return the following day, besides Laurel wanted to get to the hotel to deal with the current problem.

Prior to saying good night to Susan both David and Laurel had a quiet word with her because the behaviour displayed was uncharacteristic. Susan on the other hand felt what they did was ok. They were on the island and it was safe. Janae and George knew about the club and thought it would be a good place for them to see and of course they also thought dancing would be occurring.

"Mum we were tired waiting for you and we wanted to see the place rather than hearing about it. I guess you and Dad liked it but do you know what it was like for us sitting there listening to the history of the island?"

David and Laurel looked at each other.

"Susan we did not think of it like that, I guess we were being selfish forgetting that we had your friends in our midst nevertheless, you could have left a message for us indicating where you were going".

With a hug from both of her parents the event of the evening was dealt with and they retired to bed looking forward to further explorations the following day.

True to his word David and the group returned 'down yonder' and got a view of the Vic Hum club in the day light.

Next door to the club was Cyril who at age 85 operated a small laundry. He usually sits outside and watch for the tourists who go into the club or simply walking in the area. It was during their walk toward Barracks Hill, David, Laurel and the young people stopped briefly and he told them about the days when cricket was a social outing for the community and that he has a young man played the game as well. While capturing their attention, Cyril also gave them a little history on himself as a younger man. Not only was he involved in the game but he worked as a carpenter and built many houses on that island. He was also known for building one of the eleven Super Value Food Stores, Golden Gates in Nassau. Additionally in those days he also was responsible for making coffins and arranging the deceased in it prior to the final resting place. There was much laughter surrounding that particular task because he shared how a coffin was made too small so he had to break the legs of the deceased to fit the body in the coffin.

Feeling Susan togging on his shirt, David knew she had enough of that tale and they continued towards Barracks Hill. They had to visualize that it was a cricket ground because it now was well developed with dwelling houses and back yard gardens.Inclusive of that view they saw the harbour and while standing there they were approached by a former Chief Councillor, Eloise Knowles who lived in the subdivision and she pointed out what is known as the 'point' and it is a look out spot for seeing the arrival of the fast ferry, the Day Break or in yester years the Air Swift which was the local mail boat.

Driving along the main street in Harbour Island, David, Laurel and the youngsters came to the famous fig tree which is a landmark on the island. Pulling out his brochure, which was compiled by the Ministry of Tourism, David shared that the tree withstood many hurricanes and it is found on many poster cards and paintings. It is included in the golf cart tours organised by The Bahamas Fast Ferries and known as the 'The Fig Tree Park—famous as a meeting place for all the seaman and farmers, where they discussed life in Harbour Island. In August 1992 hurricane Andrew destroyed the original popular tree which had stood for more than 75 years'.

Among all the varying professions on the island, boat building was very popular. Many boats including the Dart which was the 'first regular Family Island Mail Boat was said to have been a small two-mast schooner . . . sailing between Nassau and Harbour Island in 1870. In the 1800's Dunmore Town became a noted shipyard and sugar refinement centre, which gave the islanders an all important industry. The shipyard, renowned for shipbuilding, built the Marie J. Thompson, a four masts schooner in 1922 which 'was the queen of them all, being 696 tons in size, she remains the largest ship ever built in The Bahamas . . . sailed to Key West, New York and the Carolinas in record time and took coconuts, sugar cane and pineapples in reasonable amounts'.

Some of the sugar cane was processed on the island at that time. 'Hoppie Higgs and Joseph Albury established three small sugar mills which processed sugar cane for inter-island trade and local consumption'.

David found this hard to believe and the young people marvel at what they had learnt particularly when they considered the distance and to think that people travelled by sailed boat. Other notable mail boats inclusive of the Noel Roberts and Gary Roberts which was built much later also had their genesis in Harbour Island.

Susan found this information exciting and tried to imagine boat building on the current landscape. Her father who was recalling some of the information he obtain from Prince during their chat the previous evening however assured her that such action did take place.

Finding the drive a relief because she was able to get some cool breeze, Laurel encouraged David to locate a restaurant where they could experience Briland cuisine. He remembered seeing Star Fish Restaurant while they drove through Barracks Hill and everyone agreed that they could try it. Angela the owner of the restaurant greeted them warmly and gave them a brief history of her establishment. She was established since 1962 and was famous for seafood and native dishes. Susan and her friends were happy with that and prior to arriving at the restaurant they already plotted to have cracked conch with peas and rice. David and Laurel both had a good laugh because to them the young people were always a step ahead of them.

The meal was completed with coconut tart and by that time everyone wanted to rest and later go to the beach. This of course would be Laurel first time going to the Pink Sand Beach. What would be her view?

Chapter 25

S ettling on the veranda of the hotel, Janae, George and Susan reflected on what they had seen so far on 'Briland'. George was impressed but felt that they should be able to do more on their own.

"Susan I know your parents are very protective of all of us but we could do a lot more by ourselves. I heard there is a club called Seagrapes not too far from here. Do you think they would let us go there"?

"I agree with you George but my parents especially my mother is very timid and always thinks the worst, let me see what I can do once they have their rest. Maybe I could ask them while we go to the beach".

Janae was less optimistic and felt they better be satisfied with the current arrangement.

"Hello, I am Lydia, my job is to help to entertain young people like yourselves. Have you heard of the Regatta that takes place each year in October?"

Janae and George were aware of this activity but it was new to Susan and she immediately wanted Lydia to tell her more about it. George somewhat bored wanted to know about the nearby Seagrapes night club.

"Susan, let me give you a bit of history". 'Regattas including working sailboats had been held in Nassau as early as 1831'. They began to spread to the 'Out Islands', now known as 'Family Islands' 'around 1900—75 and was the brain child of J. Linton Rigg, the son of a bishop of Jamaica. A pioneer of yacht cruising in The Bahamas, Rigg retired from his New York ship brokering business in his forties to live on what was then isolated Goat Cay, Great Exuma, and indulge full-time in his fanatical love of sailing . . . Filling an evident need, the Family Island Regatta . . . became an annual event from 1981 . . . some 18 regattas on 15 islands are now held each year'.

"I am sure all of this is not new to Janae being an island girl but George I hope you got something from it. Oh and let me tell you what was the purpose of the regatta when it first started": 'to sustain Bahamian boatbuilding and sailing skills and provide spice of competition, but at the same time to occasion an annual party, at which Bahamians of all sorts and visitors from all over mingle peacefully and in friendship'.

"Lydia the purpose of the regatta is a great idea. I can see the skill of sailing is still going on but what about boat building? During our tour of the island we saw the spot where boats use to be built but that is no more, so how is that other part of the purpose for regatta is met?" asked Susan.

"Well, it is not met here in 'Briland' and I am not sure what happens on the other islands but I believe there is still some boat building in Abaco. Remember 15 islands have regattas each year".

"Never mind, tell me what happens here in 'Briland' in October".

George seems to have regained his interested in the conversation and nodded his head in agreement for Lydia to share some of that information.

"Well first of all there is a committee that meets to the plan the event. Boats from around The Bahamas for the races are brought to the island by mail boats; stalls for selling of food, arts and craft and other items of interest are rented to interested parties. These persons are mainly from Nassau and other islands or other parts of Eleuthera as well as the local community. Small boutique hotels rent rooms for the influx of guest coming for the event, night clubs and individual bands all play a major role in entertaining. Additional funding is made a few weeks prior to the event by having a cruise in the Nassau Harbour and a cook out the following day. This activity, not only make money but is also a mean of advertising the event".

"Lydia this island is so small and what you are saying a lot of people visit for this event. What is the atmosphere like?"

"Susan that is a good question. Some of the guests come without making arrangements to have a place to stay. Those persons of course prayed for good weather because what they do is sleep on the beach.'

"Sleep on the beach!!!"

"Yes that is a common practice. Remember we are a safe little island and sleeping under the stars is no problem".

Janae and George both laughed when they looked at Susan's face. She was horrified by what she heard but they felt that was part of her past. Her mother especially was very protective, hence Susan' life was very sheltered.

Lydia turned her attention to George's question and told him about the many night clubs around the island, including those in the major hotels but during regatta time those hotels were generally closed.

"George, if you are able to visit during that period I think you would like either Sea grapes night club which is . . . over by the library . . . it's the spot most likely to get rocking with live local music. Then there is Charlie's bar, right in the centre of town next to Arthur's bakery. Charlie's gets a loyal following of locals and travellers from Nassau".

George liked that information and immediately turned to Janae whispering. Susan saw that action and remembered her recent encounter with her mother.

"Count me out of that one George. I don't know what you are planning".

Both Janae and George laughed mischievously at Susan's remark. She would have to wait and see what their next move would be.

"Susan, Janae and George, did you have a good rest and are your ready for the beach", shouted Laurel.

They did not rest at all but going to the beach was perfect. This would be their last swim before heading back to South Eleuthera. Without giving an answer, they quickly met David and Laurel in the foyer. During the short ride to the beach they told them about their chat with Lydia and that they should make plans to return to 'Briland' during the month of October when the Regatta occurs.

The tide was low which gave them the opportunity to walk a distance to meet the sea. David warned them to be careful because the tide comes in quickly some time. Meanwhile Laurel was captivated by the pinkness of the sand and reflected on how it is known all over the world. One theory states that 'the sand is due to a coral insect, which lives on the reefs (the devil's backbone is one such reef), which has a pink body. After the insects die, the wave action crushes the bodies and washes the remains ashore and mixes it in with the sand'. Laurel was not keen about going into the water, she stayed with David under the thatched roof shed and marvelled at the beauty of the environs.

While enjoying the view they reflected on what it must have been like to have items drifting on to the beach from ship wrecked ships. From their research they were made aware of this trade which dated back to the 1800's. 'The crossroads of many sailing routes, The Bahamas was notorious for its uncharted rocks and shoals, which multiplied the normal dangers of unexpected changes of wind weather and the occasional storms . . . Wrecks were positive godsends to the impoverished islanders. They offered chances of obtaining materials not produced in the islands and the opportunity of selling rescued cargoes'.

'Almost as much as pirates, Bahamian wreckers gained a fearsome reputation, but were in fact victims of poverty and necessity rather than . . . being callous brutes . . . Certain strategically located islands and settlements became notorious as bases for wreckers, such as Bimini for the Florida Strait, Ragged Island for the Old Bahama Channel and north Cuban shore, Long Cay for the Crooked Island Passage, and Rock (previously Wreck) Sound Eleuthera for Central Bahamas'.

David and Laurel both concluded that for "Briland' the wrecking near Rock Sound was the key and as a result the locals benefitted but with the establishment of lighthouses and improved navigational aids 'wrecking had virtually died out by the twentieth century'.

Not wanting to wait to late before they visit a few more places, David went to the water's edge to get the young people out of the water. They thought they could visit the Anglican

Church, stop in and have a look at Coral Sands and finally try to locate the alley where the bread maker of the old days resided and baked bread in a brick oven.

Walking into the St John's Anglican Church, Laurel and her group tried to visualize what it must have been like many years ago. It is the 'oldest religious foundation in The Bahamas dating back to 1768. The Loyalist worshipped as early as the mid 1700's. History also revealed that the Eleutherian Adventurers in 1647 migrated there and it is assumed that their descendents would have been living when this Church was erected'.

George was amazed to know that they could be standing in such an edifice. David however reminded them that some repairs were done over the years because several times hurricanes damaged the roof.

Passing the Methodist Church they quickly went to Coral Sands just to have a peek. Like Pink Sand Hotel they heard a lot about this established and did not want to leave the island without seeing it. From the casual glance it looked very stylish. Speaking with one of the staff members they were informed that it was recently renovated and its British colonial style was attributed to renowned interior designer Barbara Hulanicki. The rooms were said to be elegant and luxurious, located on 8 tropical acres lushly landscaped grounds.

Graciously thanking the staff they hurriedly left to find the small alley way that lead to the former home of the late Naomi

Fisher. She too was involved in the tourist industry and in addition to that job she supplied fresh baked bread for the island. From the research that David had done on this baker, she rose early in the morning to prepare the mixture and wood for the fire which was burnt in a brick oven. Early every morning her customers could be assured that they would have their hot bread and again later in the day another batch would be prepared. In those days the bread was displayed in a shop called Ms. Mae Shop and latter years she sold it in Tip Top Shop. Being a Native American, in her sunset years she returned to the land of her birth and for a while her daughter Agnes Kemp continued her trade of producing fresh baked bread for the community.

Susan commented to her parents that it must have been difficult to bake bread in that manner because it meant that there always had to be a supply of wood to create the fire. Nevertheless she felt that their trip to the North was great and along with Janae and George they were looking forward to going home to South Eleuthera. What would be next for Susan as she gets use to island life?

Chapter 26

"What a week it has been, David and it seems like we have been away from our home for ages", said Laurel.

"I agree with you and I am happy to be back. Where is Susan? She is sleeping late today. I hope she has not gone into one of those moods".

Heavy footsteps were heard coming towards the kitchen and to Laurel ears, she did not like what she was hearing.

"Susan is that you?" she shouted.

Barely hearing a mumble both David and Laurel together went into the corridor and to their amazement Susan face told the story. Yes she was in one of those moods. David as usual sprung into action and hugged her, hoping that she would relax and tell them what was on her mind. Unfortunately it took a bit more probing before he could get her to open up.

"I don't want to go to boarding school any more".

The statement from her was cause for alarm. They had already made the final arrangements, they had no other school selected and this now came as a complete shock to them. What caused her to change her mind because prior to the trip she was excited and happy to be on her own? This called for a family meeting. David pulled out a chair at the table and all of them set down so they could have a discussion to determine what brought about this decision.

Listening to Susan's explanation, she felt that since spending those days with Janae and George, they both seemed to be so much more matured than she was, knew a lot of information about the world (so she thought) and that she needed to be more knowledgeable about travel and people.

David who always thought she was matured for her age could not understand this and felt that it was more to what she was telling them.

"Susan, your mum and I are trying to get to the bottom of your decision. Did something happen that we are not aware of? Remember you agreed to go to boarding school even before we discussed it, so what made you change your mind?"

"Sighing loudly . . . George mentioned about me being his special girl. I don't want to be his special girl and if I go to school in the States where he is going, I would have to be his special girl. Janae heard him saying this and she did not help me but gave a big, big laugh".

Laurel opened her eyes wide and gave David that 'told you so look', but David being the jolly person that he was and the fact that his daughter was grappling with information common to teenagers was not put off by his wife. Motioning Laurel to leave them alone, David wanted to speak with Susan on his own. David loved his daughter and read widely about being the proper Dad. He knew that 'the father is the first man in the life of . . . a girl and he plays an important role'. It is most likely for this reason he paid a lot of attention to Susan, although at times it may appear that both he and Laurel were over protective.

Lovingly he explained to Susan what George statement could possible mean. He also made a mental note to discuss with Laurel the need for them to talk to Susan about relationships because she was an adolescent and would soon become attracted to the opposite sex.

Meanwhile Laurel was busy in the kitchen but was also reflecting on what she had discussed with David in 'Briland' about being more positive regarding Susan. She was determined to play a more meaningful role in her life especially now that she is going through adolescence. Like David she too read so that she could influence Susan to be the best that she can be and now she feels more than ever, the knowledge gained is of the utmost importance. Recognising that she 'need to mentor . . . her, but not as if . . . she was coaching her to win a beauty contest . . . should provide the down-to-earth perspective . . . she needs when she get buffeted by comparisons, competition, faltering confidence, and classroom spitefulness'. By Susan's own admission she revealed to her parents that her confidence was faltered by the comments made by George.

Hearing footsteps Laurel turned towards the door and saw David's calm face, which indicated to her that all was well.

"You know David you have such a way with handling Susan. What was your answer to her concern?"

"Laurel you know that we have both been preparing ourselves for this time in her life and so I simply tried to get her to see the comment in a positive light. Remember I told you that we have to give her some credit for what happens in her life and I think this occasion was the beginning. Once she listened and understood what was said, she brightened up and promised to be more analytical when she receives information. The idea of not going to boarding school has been resolved and she is refocused on preparing to journey with Janae and George".

"I am happy about that but I am determined to spend more time with her so that we can strengthen that mother/daughter bond. Laurel hope that this would, empower her to be more and more independent and gain that confidence that will be needed when she moves away".

Resolving that crisis was timely. Nina appeared at the door wanting to catch up on the details of the trip. David let her in and was happy to escape and leave them two to talk but he found himself walking and meeting up with George father,

Ian. Although wanting some quiet time to reflect on Susan he welcome his friend and they both strolled towards the centre of the settlement where they too talked about the trip to the North and at the same time reviewed the plans for travelling to the Boarding School. David being very careful to not divulge his recent concern with Susan, he said how they all were looking forward to the arrangement and that once she is settled, Laurel and himself will visit family in the UK for a short while and later visit North Long Island.

David also took that opportunity to discuss the state of affairs with young men in the community and to get Ian's view on what is the likely activity that could be beneficial to them. What he learnt was that there were a number of young men who lacked the support of their fathers but also found out that his friend was a strong advocate for the community to be involved. He was happy about this stance because he had read an article 'Why Communities have a stake in raising our Boys' sometime ago and the conversation caused him to remember it. The major points were highlighted and David noted the identified issues: 'For safety—because boys turn their frustration outward . . . crime, violence; For girls—boys misplaced aggression will carry it into their relationships with other people including girls—throughout their lives; For . . . society . . . trouble boys will turn away from service, honourable activity and work to create problems rather than to solve them . . . they will come to believe that they are worthless'.

Ian was listening intensely to David and agreed with him that the factors he mentioned were key and as a community, they should address them so that the large number of young men that sit under the tree can become productive citizens. Together they felt that the re-introduction of Boy's Brigade, Sports and one-on-one dialogue with the young men will be a start. They also recognised that other men inclusive of pastors must be involved however, they will spearhead the activity.

At last, after that conversation, David was able to be alone with his thoughts. He truly believed that his wife must now play a more prominent role in Susan life and he pull back. Yes, he understood Laurel being disappointed because of what they have experienced in the past but all is not lost. He can see that Mrs. Forbes, the social worker, believes that Susan can overcome her issues with the strong support of her family especially her mother. Attending boarding school will truly be a test for her because for one, she would be a long distance from home and she would have to dig deep within her own resources to solve challenges that would come her way.

Arriving back at home he was happy to know that Susan had ventured out to be with Janae and Laurel was beginning to sort out her clothing for the trip. Boarding school is now on the radar or is it still a challenge?

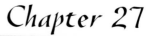

Chapter 27

Well there was no more concerns expressed by Susan and all of the families were ready to travel to the US. For Susan and her friends they were all attending the same school and this made the arrangement easy for them.

The three young people were very happy and for Laurel that observation made her feel comfortable leaving Susan because their focus would be on returning to the UK for a short period. The other parents, like the typical Bahamians would spend an additional week for some shopping.

Susan made it easy for her parents to say good bye and for this reason they had no difficulty in leaving her three days after their arrival. However Laurel still had some reservations regarding George. She hoped that the recent time spent with Susan and the fact that they talked about a number of issues relating to relationships would be remembered and she would rise above her initial concerns. David, on the other hand, was more confident and told his wife to let the matter rest and for them to enjoy their first trip aboard without Susan, resting assured that she was safe at her school.

Arriving at Heathrow, both David and Laurel were happy to be back at home. Laurel, taking her husband's advice purposely made it a point to enjoy the trip and to see as much of her old home town as possibly.

She was amazed at the new terminal five at Heathrow and delighted that it was established because prior to the new structure, travelling at the previous terminals was congested. The atmosphere was delightful and she barely heard David telling her that she would be further surprised when she saw the departure lounge; it was set up like a shopping mall with several high end stores and restaurants.

Not having an agenda of her own, Laurel followed her husband in visiting the Grand Lodge in Scotland. He also wanted to visit, Perth, Australia and Singapore. At first, they re-established themselves at their home, connected with relatives and friends via telephone and in the mean time planned their various trips.

After being in Eleuthera, they both became accustomed to the native sweet potato, plantain and cassava. Laurel knew she would find those items at the Brixton market. Wanting to travel alone so she could truly browse, she left David at home and walked to Park Lane to catch the number 73 bus. It took about twenty-five minutes to get to Brixton but at the same time she would be seeing familiar sights, especially looking down from the top deck of the bus.

A visit to the Brixton market was a must to get the Caribbean foods that they craved. The market made her reflect on her school history where they were taught about the 'Windrush Generation' who in 1948 'the first wave of immigrants (492 individuals) . . . arrived on the Empire Windrush from Jamaica . . . and spread out into local accommodations. The ship was en route from Australia to England via the Atlantic, docking in Kingston Jamaica. An advertisement had appeared in a Jamaican newspaper offering cheap transport on the ship to anybody who wanted to work in Britain.' From what she remembered some of them became bus conductors.

Although she previously lived in the UK, Brixton was not an area familiar to Laurel and initially she was confused when she got off the bus. However, she looked around and the market was directly in front of her.

The variety of fruit and vegetables was an eye-opener for Laurel and she was able to obtain her items as well as mangoes and avocadoes. Continuing to browse she went into a fish market where there were friendly staff who no doubt knew their trade and skilfully engaged customers and seem to generated alot sales.

Amazed that the trip brought up those memories, Laurel felt that she had spent enough time in the market and strolled towards the bus stop for the return journey. She had a lot to tell David and maybe the next time they can go together.

One day while walking towards South Audley Street, very near the American Embassy, to their surprise they saw the name 'Baha Mar' and upon closer inspection realized that it was a model of the project taking shape in western New Providence. The real estate agent Hampton was the PR for the company in London.

"David, this is great. You remember a few weeks ago there was some information on the news about this, yes in a news release they announced West Bay Street opening and handing over ceremony", said Laurel.

"That's right Laurel, from what I understood the company rerouted the old West Bay Street and constructed a new street. There was even talk about it on the talk shows because this company only took nine months and the other company that is working on the inner city streets is taking a much longer time. Additionally the Prime Minister is now thinking that he could get 'Baha mar' engineers to help. Anyway what all this means is that we will have good roads to drive on when we next go to Nassau and of course by that time I will be driving'.

They both recognised that with publicity here in London most likely other compatriots would be joining them in The Bahamas.

Being very near to the Bahama House, they called on the High Commissioner who had just finished a busy week of activities with the International Maritime Organisation (IMO). He is the permanent representative for The Bahamas and for the last two years served as Vice President of the General Assembly. He was happy to see them and most of all to share his success regarding The Bahamas being re-elected to Category 'C' one of the classifications within the organisation. They listened enthusiastically as he told them of the campaign that they mounted and how their evenings were spent going from one reception to another just to ensure that they got the required votes.

David and Laurel were happy to see him and they too, shared their adventure to Harbour Island and how they were intrigued with the Vic Hum Club and most of all how they met his father-in-law and they could not forget to mention Prince, the historian. Together they shared how knowledgeable he was about his beloved island.

Although they would have loved to stay and hear more about the High Commissioner's trip to Perth and Singapore, they did not want to spoil their own visit to those countries by knowing too much in advance. He however did mention that Singapore in particular was a beautiful city prior to wishing them well during the remainder of their visit.

Passing Grosvenor Chapel, Laurel could not resist the temptation of walking inside. Nothing had changed. At the entrance was the usual notices and list for upcoming activities. She realized that they had an interim priest because the former one had been elevated to Chancellor at the St Paul's Cathedral in the city. Knowing that David had been patient with her, she finally made her exit and together they walked to The Grill at the Dorchester Hotel for lunch. At the entrance, they saw that the hotel was celebrating eighty years of service to the Mayfair community. The number was made from the growth of beautiful luscious red and green flowers. It was truly a land mark and what they could see, it was still popular. The atmosphere in the restaurant was pleasant and the food of excellent quality. There was a jovial group in the corner having a wonderful time. From all appearances it looked like they were saying farewell to one of their colleagues. There were speeches and exchange of a gift.

After such a sumptuous lunch they returned home to check emails. Laurel promised to email Susan every day and rushing out during the morning, she had forgotten to do so. This was her way of trying to maintain contact or was it more trying to control. Thinking over this point gave her food for thought. It seemed like she was having a difficult time letting go in comparison to David. He seems to be very calm and always upbeat when any mention is made of Susan especially in reference to her attending boarding school. Reflecting on Nina's comments, Laurel knew that she has to wean herself from her daughter and trust that the values instilled at home guided her as she continued to develop into adult hood.

David noticing the pensive look on Laurel's face called out to her:

"Laurel, why the glum face, we are here to enjoy ourselves and to celebrate our achievement in nurturing Susan thus far".

"David that is so true but you know I still need some time to get used to the idea that my baby has flown the nest and is making her own way in boarding school. I guess you being the father see it differently from me. But you know I was just here pondering over it and telling myself to get over it".

"Oh Laurel, I know it is hard but I would try my best to assist you and together we would move beyond this point".

"Thanks David, I am so happy you said that, you're such an inspiration to me".

Later in the evening, Laurel attempted to send an email to Susan, only to find that the internet connection at the home was not working. She decided not to get anxious but to stay calm because there was not anything that she could do at the moment. She realized that the next day she could go to the library near Grosvenor Chapel and use their computer. Smiling to herself, she recognised how fortunate it was for members of the community to have access to technology and looked forward to the day when a similar arrangement could be accessible in Eleuthera.

David interrupted her thoughts. He just came off the telephone and was disappointed. The arrangement for going on their trip would be cut short because the airline would not be able to get them back to London in time to catch their flight to The Bahamas.

"But David it will not be worth it to travel 18 hours for 7 days and what about Singapore, we will not be able to stop over".

"I know Laurel and that is why I have not yet confirmed what we will do. What do you think? Do you really believe it would be a waste of time going for the 7days? I think it is worth it and that we should go. Why not, we are on holiday. Think about it, we have until tomorrow to confirm with the agency".

Laurel reviewed what David and said and guessed that it would be okay; she just needed to relax and enjoy travelling to that part of the world, any way she will sleep on it and talk to David in the morning.

Prior to getting out of bed they again discussed their trip and agreed that they would go. Meanwhile Laurel would prepare breakfast and later go to the library to use the computer. She needed to hear from Susan so that she could be assured that she had settled into the routine of the school.

The library was not open, looking more closely at her watch Laurel realized that she had left home to early and she had a twenty minute wait. Walking back to the corner, she chatted with the flower vendor who told her that his business was brisk and he was happy that he selected that spot. It also was the main road to St. George's school and that he gets a large number of sales from parents who go to collect their children.

The minutes flew by and glazing up from her conversation with the vendor she saw that the doors to the library were open. Being the first one in she was able to use her old library card and log into the system. Sure enough there were four emails from Susan, all questioning their whereabouts and why they did not answer her emails. Additionally she told her that she was pleased with the school and already made some new friends and looked forward to hearing from them.

Laurel was over the moon. She heard from her daughter she was ok which meant that Laurel felt more comfortable to go on a trip. Walking quickly back to the home she happily told David that all was well with Susan and with that news he agreed that they confirm their booking for the weekend. Excitement was high, Laurel and David was off on an international trip by themselves. Would they encounter any surprises? Would Susan continue to do well?

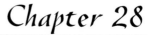

Chapter 28

*E*ighteen hours of flying was not a journey Laurel had looked forward too, but the flight attendances were friendly, there was a variety of movies. She had also brought a good book with her. Gazing lovely at her sleeping husband, she snuggled down in her seat for the remaining two hours of the flight. They had waited one hour in Singapore before commencing the final five hours to Perth which went by so quickly. David didn't have a chance to sleep so they were able to finalize the places they wanted to visit. Living at the Pan Pacific Hotel was convenient because it was located near the city centre.

The hour taxi ride from the airport allowed them to see some of city. However, talking with the driver to get a better sense of Perth was futile. He was not very communicative and appeared that he only wanted a job. What a shame commented Laurel to David. He too was surprised to the non responsive attitude.

Check in was not bad although a large number of persons were checking in. We found out that it was the Commonwealth Heads of Government Meeting (CHOG) held every two years.

To our surprise, the Queen would attend and will officially open the event. Further information revealed from the hotel, that she would also be at a banquet in the hotel. Of course, that was excitement for me but David seems to be quite nonchalant.

Apart from the shopping, David and I had agreed to go by ferry to Rottnest Island and Fremantle. Both of those visits would give us a good view of what Perth is all about. The ferry ride along the Swan River was very pleasant and after leaving the entrance to the river the ferry went into the open sea to make the crossing to Rottnest Island.

Chatting with the tour sales lady, David found out that the island was famous for its beaches, it was 'a car free zone' and other touristic activities. This was similar to The Bahamas—snorkelling, diving, surfing and swimming. Following a bus tour and after having a nice island lunch they visited the Chapel, one of the historic sites on the island. The Priest—in-charge has been on the island for the past 50 years. Another site that is treasured by the island is The Lodge 'a former Aboriginal Prison known as The Quod' but now used as a small hotel. On their return to the ferry dock David drew Laurel's attention to the Salt Store, located at the Centre of Thomson Bay Settlement. The store 'is one of the oldest building on the Island, constructed by Aboriginal prisoners in 1868 . . . and originally used to hold the bagged salt collected from the two Rottnest Island Salt Lakes, ready for transportation to Fremantle'. He pointed out to her that it was currently used as a gallery space with . . . unique art and photography exhibitions.

The return trip to Perth especially crossing the ocean was rough causing the ferry to rock. However once inside the harbour and sailing along Swan River, there was no problem.

Knowing that time moves quickly when on vacation, David made plans for their next visit—Fremantle. Their main focus would be the maritime museum although there are a lot of touristic attractions in that section of Western Australia.

Fremantle is a twenty minute drive from Perth and it is a multi-cultural City with an attractive market. It also had a beer brewery in the heart of the city. David and Laurel took a brief tour of that facility before moving on to the Maritime Museum where they saw a very unique and unusual structure which David believed that it was built in that manner to accommodate the exhibits. The structure overlooks the Indian Ocean and it is said that the 'Museum inspires visitors to discover more about Western Australia affinity with the ocean'. During the guided tour, David and Laurel were informed that included in the Museum is 'leisure boats and homemade vessels, handcrafted sailing boats, and that it is home to the winning American's Cup Yacht and an Oberon class submarine'.

"What a wonderful experience, David and I am happy that you chose that museum for us to visit and to actually see a submarine, we would have to share the visit with Susan".

"I agree with you Laurel, and I wonder if something like this would one day be built in the Bahamas. They should preserve some of those boats that they use for regatta. Never mind, let us go find a taxi to take us to the local fish restaurant before making our journey back to Perth".

After finishing a wonderful meal and the short journey into Perth, they spent the rest of the evening in the town centre because it was late night shopping.

Upon arriving in their room, there was a message for them. Laurel immediately got really worried because she was still adjusting to the idea of her little girl away to school on her own. Hearing his daughters voice at the other end of the phone was a relief and he nonverbally communicate that to Laurel, who then eagerly wanted to talk as well.

They were both happy to know that she was well because they were enjoying their trip and David in particular did not truly focus on his daughter. He felt she was okay and was of the view that they, as parents, must adapt to the fact that she is not with them and they now have an empty nest. Once she finishes high school, she would go to college so they have to get use to her no longer being in the home. If only he could get Laurel to think like that and for them to enjoy this time of their lives. Exhausted she was fast asleep while he watched his favourite movie and enjoyed the ambience of their hotel room because this was their final night in the Pan Pacific Hotel.

Breaking their trip for two days in Singapore was too short, after all it's a large city but circumstances forced them to shorten their visit and return to London for the flight to The Bahamas. Nevertheless, they made the most of the two days. Making use of the city tour was one way to get a bird's eye view of the city, browse through several malls and have a delicious dinner on the harbour side where they were able to see the beautiful lighting effects.

Singapore is a cosmopolitan city with three sections—China Town, Little India and Historic Malay area and big on tourism. It is crowded with high rises, museums, and historic buildings which were pointed out during the city tour. Their land mark Sands Hotel top floor is shaped like a boat, a very unique structure. David and Laurel also found out that they believed in green spaces and that there were over four hundred parks including a very large botanical garden.

Because they were anxious to return to The Bahamas, David and Laurel did not mind the short stay and looked forward to arriving in Eleuthera. Laurel was looking forward to resuming her work in the community and David to commence his project with George's father. Now that he had committed to the venture, he was excited and told Laurel that he could not wait to meet with the disadvantaged young men in the settlement. Would the excitement last? They would soon find out.

Chapter 29

Overnight in the Hilton Hotel at the Heathrow Airport, David sat for awhile in the lounge listening to the music while Laurel was resting from the twelve hour flight from Singapore. This was important to her and she was angry at David because he did not embrace the opportunity. The following day they would be travelling for another nine hours on the direct flight to Nassau.

David did not mind Laurel being a bit upset and sometimes he likes to be by himself to think. The music was soothing and he had an occasion to speak with other men who maybe were like him—escaping the shape tongue of their wives.

Tipping gently into the room at midnight, he felt it was enough time to get a nap. His intention was to sleep most of the time on the flight, hence the other reason for him ignoring Laurel's request for an early night.

The hotel shuttle left on time and very soon, they were in the departure lounge. While waiting for Laurel to select a cafe to have breakfast, David made several calls from his mobile to his UK friends, informing them of their early departure. In the distance he could see Laurel motioning him to come and have breakfast. Of course he agreed and ended his conversation very quickly and was happy to know that she finally selected a cafe. He ordered his favourite—full English breakfast, while she ordered her oats and fruit. So disciplined he thought to himself. He needed to start paying attention to his diet in the same manner. On his last visit to his doctor he warned him about the amount of weight he had put on and he reassured him he would start an exercise routine. Well! He is still waiting to get started despite the fact that Laurel tries to encourage him to walk on the community park.

"David, they have given us a seat near the exit. We have to get them to change with another couple". David had no problem with the arrangement but if he wanted to keep the dialogue going between them he would have to go along with the idea.

"Excuse me, we would like to change our seats if possible. My wife is not happy being in this row", said David.

"No problem, once every one is in their seats I will see what I can do".

Reclining in the premier economy section, David and Laurel waited for the flight attendant to return as promised and sort them out. Much to his surprise, she must have forgotten; the door was shut and they began to demonstrate the safety features on the plane. This did not go down well with Laurel however David could see that she was trying to be patient. After getting the attention of the head stewardess, they were eventually moved to a more suitable area and he could hear his wife sighing with relief.

Settling in to watch a movie, Laurel glanced at David who was already sleeping. He is not good company when they were flying. Now that Susan is no longer travelling with them, she thought he could at lease stay awake for awhile to keep her company. The flight attendant made up for that. Thank goodness for the flight attendant, she was able to talk sometimes otherwise, the movies, novel and crossword puzzles occupied her time during the nine hour flight.

While stretching her legs in the serving section of the plane, she met Pauline who was on her way to The Bahamas. Her husband was working on a big project there and she was going for a visit. Upon hearing that Laurel and her family's moved to The Bahamas, Pauline was eager to learn more about the island where they were living. She even hinted to Laurel that it might be a good idea for her to share that information with her husband because the project would not be completed at least for the next three to four years. Commuting to her husband was not a good alternative, especially the number of hours in the air every six weeks.

"Pauline why not encourage your husband to visit us in Eleuthera. We could talk with him and answer any questions he may have if you think he would be serious about relocating".

"That is a very good suggestion Laurel and I would try my best to persuade him to do so, after all it is me who has to do the travelling. He only comes home if he has vacation. I am excited about this plan and we must stay in contact via email".

Selecting a fruit and a drink, Laurel made her way back to her seat. She was in excellent spirits after standing for awhile and focused her attention on finding solutions to several puzzles, while reflecting on the 'bumpiness' of the flight. Just a minute ago, it was smooth when she was conversing with Pauline; that changed quickly to the extent that the captain put on the seat belt sign. David did not seem to be affected by the rough atmosphere and stirred a little but did not awake fully. He truly is something else.

Not fazed by the bumpiness in the flight she eventually gave up working on the puzzles and to turn her attention to her own concerns. She recognised recently that she had been very 'short' with David and knew that it was to do with her not wanting Susan to go to boarding school but David seemed to have no difficulty with it. Was she fearful of the empty nest syndrome? Nina gave her advice but she did not think Susan going to school would affect her. Lately she found herself being sad and feelings of losing her daughter. Right away, she knew it was not a good sign and did not know how to tell David about this new twist in her life. Would he listen to her or brush it off like he sometimes does? In her reflective mood, she remembered reading that one should not be ashamed, so with that view point she made up her mind to have a discussion with David.

"Ah, David it is good to have you awake for a change. You always leave me to fend for myself when we travel, but it also gave me chance to think about my feelings relative to Susan attending the boarding school. Of course that was nothing new to you. I have determined that the 'empty nest syndrome' caught up with me".

"Empty nest syndrome, come on Laurel! Any way since you believe that, I am happy to know that you recognised your problem and hopefully are ready to let it go so together we could re-establish our relationship. Yes. I noticed that you were irritable with me, yet I tried to be patient. By the way I hope you did not burden Susan with your feelings. Just tell her you miss her but keep how you feel to yourself, remember she too is trying to find her feet".

"Thanks David, you're always so understanding".

So deeply engrossed in that conversation, neither of them realized that they were preparing to land in Nassau. The flight was on time and they had sufficient time to catch the shuttle to the other side of the airport. The usual arrangement was made for them to catch Pineapple Air to Rock Sound. It seem like they were away for ages. What would they find awaiting them at home?

Chapter 30

Wow! David it is good to be home because it seems like we were away so long.

"Was that a knock at the door, David"?

"Laurel, Rachel is here".

Rachael, what is she doing here? We only just got in the door. Sometime friends in the settlement can be inconsiderate.

"Hi Rachel, good to see you, we just got home", said Laurel.

"Laurel, I am so sorry to come to you at this time but I knew you were not aware that Nina is in hospital".

"In hospital Nina, what happen?"

"Dengue fever".

While travelling both David and Laurel heard that there was an unusual outbreak in Nassau but how did Nina get it?

Rachel reading their faces quickly told them about Nina spending two weeks in Nassau with her family and about two weeks after she returned home she began to experience the flu-like symptoms. This thing is really ragging in Nassau, so much so that the 'U.S. Embassy . . . issued an emergency message for U.S. citizens in The Bahamas . . . 'Of course David and Laurel vaguely knew about the dengue fever based on information they gathered from the African Countries. Now they realized it is also in The Bahamas, Caribbean, and the Americas, all of which are tropical or subtropical and transmitted by aedes mosquito and not passed on by human beings.

"That information David is good for us to know, however I wish we had known before coming to Eleuthera. We could have visited her in the hospital" said Laurel.

"Rachel, we are so sorry to hear this news, but keep us up dated on her progresses".

Laurel after hearing that news she turned her attention to unpacking while David tried to reach Susan on the phone. They both were anxious to hear from her and it felt like it was ages since they heard her voice. Hearing David talking and laughing she quickly joined him in the living room. His expression revealed that all was well with Susan however, she wanted to hear for herself what had been happening for the past month. Later she said to David that their daughter seem to adjust to her new school and not once did she mentioned missing home. They both were also pleased that she was not emotional which gave them greater confidence that the worst of that behaviour was over. Just before their trip, Ms Forbes, the social worker had visited them at home making inquiries about her well being and told them she believed the schooling overseas would be advantageous for her well being.

Laurel got her first call from the high school to commence her sessions again with the children. Shortly afterwards she was asked to speak at the Parent Teachers Association (PTA) in Palmetto Point. David taking the queue from his wife made contact with Ian because just before leaving the island they had agreed to develop a programme to address the needs of the young men.

To David's surprise, Ian had done a lot of work while he was away. Already there was a tennis group meeting every Saturday in Tarpum Bay where both boys and girls attend for the morning hours and on Friday nights he had compiled a list of young men to meet in the Anglican Church. David agreed with Ian's format whereby they would initially have an open forum and from there sieve out the issues which were most important to the boys. They recognised that they had to move cautiously so that the attendees would not drift away and at the same time spread the word and encourage others to join. Secondly, the sessions had to be entertaining because the young men like youngsters everywhere got bored quickly.

This was great news for Laurel, she really wanted David to find something to get involved with. Work in the community was perfect. She was very excited and already had some ideas that she wanted to share with him and Ian. Laurel was a firm believer of the African proverb: 'it takes a village to raise a child'. While she tried to change the behaviour one child at a time at school, Ian and David could be trying to change the behaviour of the young adult males. With the three of them being professionals in their own right, they were aware that they had an awesome task ahead of them but nevertheless they were not daunted by it.

Looking to the future, David mentioned to Ian that the success of their model in Deep Creek could mean that they could export it to Harbour Island. His keen eye while on that island notice that a similar situation seem to be taking place with young men. They seemed to be idle for the most part although he was not certain whether it was seasonal. The suggestion was favoured by Ian who even gave themselves a target date to help them to keep focus and to have a time line to move forward.

"David, I am so proud of you said Laurel. You finally found your niche and together with Ian appear to be on to something that could boost the morale of the young men in this community and the surrounding settlements".

"Laurel I knew for months that you wanted men to be more involved but nothing happens before the time. Who is it at the door?"

"Nina, what are you doing here at this hour"?

"Laurel I need to see David urgently. I stopped at Ian's house but he was not at home".

"David! Is there a problem Nina?"

Tearfully Nina, who recently recovered from the dengue fever, was happy to see him. Upon seeing their friend Nina he tried to calm her down and tried to get her to talk to him because obviously there was a matter of grave concern.

At last, he was able to make sense of what was being said. For months Nina was hiding the fact that her teenage son, Phillip was acting out and tonight was the final straw. She had to find help because he came to fight her and threatened to burn the house down. Being very afraid she came looking for David or Ian once the young man had left the home. Further questioning reveal that he might be in a gang as well as he maybe using drugs.

Wow, that was a lot for David to take in especially since this type of behaviour was never mentioned to them during the past years of their friendship. Seeing that it was already late in the night, Laurel agreed with David that Nina could spend the night in Susan's room and tomorrow he would inform Ian about the matter and they would plan a strategy to meet with Phillip. As much as David would like to deal with it right away he realized that a cooling off period would be more beneficial at that time.

David's hunch was correct. In the morning he found out that the teenager was arrested for assaulting a police officer. His behaviour was drug induce, the police did not want to take any chances of him getting into any more trouble so they let him stay overnight in a cell. Nina upon hearing this latest event, cried but was also relieved because she strongly believe that he needs help and with him being behind bars, David and Ian could better assess his situation.

As soon as possible Ian was notified and they both visited the police station In Rock Sound. After speaking with Phillip for about an hour they both concluded that he was not a candidate for their programme and was reflecting on their next move.

Mrs. Forbes came on the scene to see if she could be of assistance to the police. David was able to get a better insight into this young man because he now found out that he was well known in the community and the drug usage was problematic for some time. Nina looking very poorly was concerned about what David thought of her and he did his best to reassure her that their relationship was still okay. The main point at this time was to get the required help for her son.

Mrs. Forbes after speaking with the Police, she found out that Phillip really battered the arresting officer. She told David and Ian that recommendation was being made for Nina's son to be sent to Sandilands Hospital, the facility with responsibility for treating drug patients. Both David and Ian were elated and did their best to show Nina that the in—patient care was the best solution and that upon his release they would be there to give supportive service to the whole family.

Nina graciously thanked David and Ian for their assistance and anxiously returned to her home, not knowing what she would find, since her son had threaten to damage the home. Would she be satisfied with the arrangement made for her son?

Chapter 31

*A*n event in the community is everybody business and this was truly the case with Nina, and the problem with her son was unknown to David and Laurel. While reflecting on what transpired they too were reminded of their own situation with Susan? They were very secretive about her unstable emotional behaviour but for all they knew that too maybe out in the community. Laurel remembered there was an occasion when they asked Janae and George to leave the home during one such episode. Did they mention it to their parents? For David and Laurel they were not dwelling on that matter but believed in their heart and in keeping with the words of Lao-Tzu (6th century BC; founder of Taoism) . . . always be on the lookout for ways to turn a problem into an opportunity for success. Always be on the lookout for ways to nurture your dream.' That was there vision for Susan and from all appearances they were well on their way to achieve it. The reports from the school so far gave no indication of any adverse behaviour. Susan, very jovially spoke with them on a regular basis and has adjusted to the boarding school environment. From all accounts her grades were excellent and it looks like she is well on her way to being a well adjusted young lady.

With the event of the previous day behind them David and Ian continued with their plans and were surprised to see the number of young men who approached them indicating their interest in the meeting for Friday evenings. Some of whom were aware of what Phillip was doing and they too dabbled in drugs. With this new information, David and Ian had to make adjustments to their programme. They were no longer dealing with young men who needed to be motivated to work but there was now the drug factor to content with. Immediately they brought Mrs. Forbes into their management team because she was acquainted with the social services and drug programmes in Nassau. They recognised that at some point they would need speakers to visit the island to share with the group the virtues of staying drug free. Meanwhile they got a telephone call from Mrs. Forbes who had alerted her counterpart at the Sandilands Hospital, Social Work Unit to keep her abreast of Phillip's progress. It would appear that he would be there for at least six months. Already she stated that he was showing some resistance but she indicated that her colleagues and the other staff at that unit know how to deal with such persons.

Laurel in the mean time was lending support to Nina who seems to be displaying guilt regarding the path her son had chosen. She was fully aware that self discrimination will not help her and appeared to be receptive to the advice Laurel and Rachel was providing. Already she had indicated to them that she would travel to Nassau so that she could speak with the doctor and therapist because she did not believe that he had to stay in hospital for six months. Nina was displaying the typical attitude of parents who protect their children in antisocial behaviour. Laurel, although saying it in love had to point out to her that she needed to allow the professionals to do their job for the sake of her son, if she wanted him to get well and lead a productive life.

Rachel was shocked to hear Nina utter such remarks, knowing full well that she had put up a lot with her son over the past year.

"What is Nina's problem? Phillip has stolen her money, damaged some of her windows and even threatened to burn down her house and she still appears to want him home before he is recovered. Laurel we really have to be firm with her and try and show her the benefit of having that boy in that facility".

'I agree whole heartily with you Rachel and I believe as a team we could get her to see that she must let those currently responsible for him do their job. This may also mean that one of us should go with her to Nassau because in her emotional state she could say the wrong thing.'

'Laurel you're right, let me think about it and I will have a word with Mrs. Forbes. She spent three years doing her social work training in Nassau and I am sure she is aware how we could go about seeing the right people at the hospital. Besides, Nina only recently overcame the dengue fever and she should not be stressing herself out over her wayward son'.

Reflecting on her conversation with Rachel over dinner she shared with David their concern. David at the same time was able to confirm what Laurel was saying. Comments from community members were an indication to him that Nina might go into Nassau and make decisions she would regret. Laurel recognised that this matter was serious and told David how it would make good sense for Rachel to accompany her to Nassau based on all that was said. How would they go about doing that without offending Nina? They both agreed that it was something they would have to sleep on.

Nina did not give them much time to think, she decided that she would travel to Nassau on the week—end. With that in mind Rachel invited herself to travel with her. Laurel on hearing the decision commended Rachel for her commitment. Mrs. Forbes gave her the name of the Assistance Director in charge of the social workers at the unit and rested assured that they would assist them.

The young men in the group were perturbed about the past event with Phillip but they were encouraged by David to see it as an example and for them to examine their own lives. Meanwhile, a social evening was planned for their meeting which would be at the basket ball court in Tarpum Bay so they could observe a game between the Tarpum Bay team and a team from Green Castle. Ian encouraged all of them to come out because he told them that they too might be able to have a team play in the next session which brought excitement to the group.

With the group up and running, David and Ian felt that they were making some progress and that their work was being talked about in other settlements. Ian shared with David his experience gained from the Methodist Church Mentorship Training Programme which was held in Tarpum Bay. He along with a group spent the entire week end at the Tarpum Bay Primary School, listening to lectures and acquiring skills to mentor teenagers. He told David when he was informed of the event he consented immediately to attend because he knew it would be relevant to their project. David was extremely pleased and felt even more assured that he had a committed partner who gave up his weekend so that he could be more effective with the young men in the group. Although he did not attend church regularly, he fully understood the need for spiritual guidance and was pleased to note that the training ended with all of the participants attending the morning service at the Methodist Church. He knew Laurel would also be proud of Ian and most likely hope his behaviour would rub off on him.

David and Laurel both now led busy lives and cherished moments when they could be alone and reflect on themselves. Lately they had heard from Susan who happily told them about a trip she took with the school to North Carolina. They visited a small school—Saint Andrews College where they were introducing students to the College environment with the hope it would be one of their choices of College. Since being away from Eleuthera

Susan became involved with playing soccer and fortunate for her this school had a girl's team and even offered her a scholarship.

"Our daughter has truly forsaken her home, said David. I really thought after her high school years she would opt to continue studies at a British university".

"David is that what you expected? I never looked at it that way. Both you and I love The Bahamas and we have conveyed this to Susan, hence there was no doubt in my mind that she would not be returning to the UK any time soon. Besides all of her friends are now in this part of the world", responded Laurel.

They both laughed at themselves knowing full well that they loved their new community and the people. Their recent concern with Nina and her son was an example and David didn't forget to mention his boys group.

Regarding the group he told Laurel how he recently read a piece in the UK Times about 'The Prince of Wales had called a meeting of Ministers and Opposition politicians to attempt to find ways of rescuing a 'lost generation' from youth unemployment'.

"That is not a bad thing David. Last week the Minister of Youth, Sports and Cultural Affairs was mentioning a similar thing here in The Bahamas. In fact they have the volunteer programme going where by persons wishing to register to volunteer their time to assist in various areas of the community; they have a fifty-two week programme going as well where selected persons were employed for that period of time; the Fresh Start Programme which provides job search, skills and training to youth between 16—25, the skills necessary for successful employment and job retention. All of this seems to be leaning towards providing necessary skills for that grouping of persons".

During this period of their reflective time David said to Laurel how Ian had participated in a church event last weekend which would help their group programme. He knew is wife would be happy for them and she sure gave a loud shout hoping that David would embrace some of the knowledge Ian had gained at church. Would she eventually see a marked change in her husband's approach to church?

Chapter 32

*T*ime surely made a difference. David himself wondered how he was now so sensitive to the well being of individuals. Was he truly emulating Ian? Recently, he found himself handling the affairs of the young men with more care. He began to recognise that despite their short coming some of them were talented. Why did he not notice it before? The experience at the Tarpum Bay Park saw a number of them showing off their skills and they concluded that they could definitely play basket ball in the next community league.

Laurel also noted this tenderness or improved sensitivity especially during the period that they meet with Nina, upon her return from seeing her son in Nassau. Prior to this meeting David had very little patience with her particularly her manner regarding how she dealt with her son's drug problem. His new approach caused him to be tolerant and even when he was tempted to scold her about berating the hospital staff he gently encouraged her to give the staff a chance to work with her son and to be supportive to them. From her account, he was a challenge to the staff and they were doing their best to provide the necessary therapy. There was a bright spot however and she was eager to share it with Laurel and David. They believed he could be released after four months and attend the remaining sessions required at the Community Counselling and Assessment Centre. This all depended on his behaviour. Both David and Laurel were happy for Nina because she now had something to look forward to.

More surprises were in store for Laurel. David expressed his desire to attend Church with her the following Sunday and she got a letter from her sister in the UK outlining the activities for the Queen's Diamond Jubilee celebrations. Like most Brits Laurel and David marvel at the length of time she has been on the throne and from the looks of it she is still going strong at 85 years of age. This should not be strange to them because it is often seen as a joke because as a country they continue to sing the national anthem which states '... long may she reign over us ... 'thus they themselves are claiming long life for her. Although the Queen had already planted a tree in honour of the event, Laurel sister wrote about The King's Troops Royal House Artillery who gave the Royal Salute which took place at Hyde Park in London. History has recorded that this 'troop was formed in 1947 by George VI, whose death led to the accession of the Queen 60 years ago'. The first snow for the winter months presented itself and from what Laurel gathered the 41-gun salute took place against the background of a snowy white ground. The High Commissioners and Ambassadors from the realm attended braving the cold weather, slipping and sliding on the frozen ground and that some of the female Commissioners were commiserating about their high heel shoes. They however were rewarded with a luncheon with the top brass of the Royal Household Calgary Regiment.

Additionally, they also heard how their former church, the Grosvenor Chapel was under renovation. They were happy to hear this because they often lamented about the need for a fresh layer of paint. Information like this caused them both to feel home sick because they know the country's rich heritage and they liked the pomp and pageantry and they wanted improvements to occur in their church.

David secretly was planning a trip for midyear especially since it would be the Olympics and they would have the pleasure of Susan accompanying them. Meanwhile he better review the plans he had developed for the young men in the group and see what they could do to support Nina when her son returns next week from Nassau.

Since attending the basket ball game in Tarpum Bay, he had arrange with Kevin to allow some of the young men to come out on a Saturday morning to learn how to play tennis and to assist the young boys in learning base ball. All of these activities seemed to have gelled well and from all account the young men look forward to the various outings. With this outcome David is anticipating that Nina's son, whenever he returns home would be able to embrace the activities of the group. Mrs Forbes and some of the mature men in the settlement have given their support to be there for him and his mother.

What is of great importance is a job and Ian is making every effort to tap the small number of business persons. So far he is waiting to hear from the project at Cotton Bay and there might be an opening at Pineapple Air for a porter position. Meanwhile construction work is booming in Harbour Island and those interested young men will be taken over there to see if they could be successful in securing a job. The main aim of the group was to keep them focused and for them to make meaningful contributions to their respective settlements. So far the meetings have proven to be positive and the knowledge gained regarding the negative impact of drugs have taken root. Many parents have praised David and Ian for the work they had done. From Nina's report her son who was the first to bring these phenomena to light is looking forward to coming out of rehab and claims that he has learnt a lot about the dangers of drug usage. Most significantly was the faces of other patients around him and listening to their stories that got them to the point that landed them in the same 'boat' with him.

David and Ian are both mindful that to change behaviour is not easy. They would truly have to insure that Phillip change his friends, if not he will be back into a life of drugs. Their main object with him was to show him 'how to achieve success, enrich . . . his life and discover . . . his life's purpose'. Keeping the group together plus keeping a keen eye on Phillip will be a challenge because the whole Bahamas is preparing for election and from what David has seen and heard from the community, it is a time when neighbours find themselves at odds with each other. David and Ian are determining to support and work with the group.

Chapter 33

*D*avid and Laurel had lived in The Bahamas for many years and are aware of the politics. For the past year the various political groups have been campaigning for the May 7th Election. They are familiar with the party colours and recently the red shirts, yellow shirts and more recently green shirts seen throughout the settlement. Rachel laughingly wanted them to commit to one of the colours but Laurel and David realized from the last election that some people get upset if you are not wearing or identifying with the right colour shirt. The Westminster System of government was known to them. They told Rachel they were able to identify with the process inclusive of the colours. In this regard they reflected on the UK and the red, blue, gold and green with many other colours signifying the independent candidates. Laurel was eager to tell her that the recent elections in the UK resulted in a coalition government between the Tories and the Lib-democrats. Both David and Laurel were still adjusting to rallies although they have been to a number of them. These gatherings introduced the candidates to the community and open offices for their operation. At the same time the rhetoric from the various parties was outlined.

Rachel on the other hand wanted to know about the coalition government and how it operated. As soon as Laurel began to explain Rachel remembered that they had something similar when the Progressive Liberal Party (PLP) first came to office on Tuesday January 10th 1967 when the then United Bahamian Party (UBP) formerly known as the Bay Street Boys and the PLP (Progressive Liberal Party) both won 18 seats of the 38 seats, 'the other two being won by Sir Randol Fawkes, for labour in over-the-hill Nassau and by the maverick Independent Sir Alvin Braynen in Harbour Island'. These two joined with the PLP and they formed the government, putting an end to many years of being governed by the UBP.

Laurel and David decided to follow the events of the upcoming election. They soon found out that there was a new candidate for their area although they had not met him. They could not vote because they were not yet citizens of The Bahamas but found the island politics exciting. They recalled the openings of the political offices and the information they were hearing on the radio, it seemed to them that in Nassau all of the parties were busy moving through that community and visiting the Family Islands. David in particular found himself listing to all of the speeches whenever he was able to get them on radio. Not only were they interested to their own community but listened to news from the other sectors of Eleuthera which all seemed to have new persons running in the respective settlements.

Registration to be eligible to vote took place in the Post Office. This was different from the UK, once you are registered from your address, you are sent the voters card and instructions for voting along with the date in the post. The hours of voting were similar and of course the long lines as well, but because there were much more people counting of the votes could take more than twenty four hours. There were no rallies and although there was some door to door contact, the number of homes made that almost virtually impossible. Information regarding plans for the new prospective candidate was garnered from the radio, television or the newspapers. When they heard that some voters expected a hand out or to see the candidate personally they found it unbelievable. Rachel, however, reminded them that this was The Bahamas and that the communities were small.

Of great significance was the third party that had developed over the past year. Ian was able to bring David up to date on the genesis of that party known as the Democratic National Alliance (DNA) lead by Branville McCartney. He told David although third parties had been around for many years, the Bahamas Democratic League lead by Etienne Dupuch around 1954, Bahamas Federation of Labour Party lead by Sir Randol Fawkes in 1959, National Democratic Party lead by Paul Adderley in 1965, Bahamas Democratic Party lead by Cassius Stuart and the Coalition for Democratic Reform lead by Hon. Bernard Nottage, this was the first time that he could remember one fielding a full slate of candidates.

"David it would seem that the young people fancy this new group. Have you been following the comments made on the talk shows, even persons from here call in to give their opinion".

"Ian I must admit that I have not been following too much but now that you have brought it to my attention I would pay more attention".

David could not wait to tell Laurel the inside scoop he had gotten on Bahamian politics. He was tickled about the fact that they refer to it as the 'silly season'. Laurel also had information for him because she had been chatting with Nina and was so impressed with the number of females in the various parties that were candidates. She told him that she would be very interested in listening to their speeches whenever they would be aired. Not wanting to be too involved but she believed in the female perspective and that they should be actively involved just as much as the male counterpart.

"Laurel, said David, this is a new side I am seeing of you; are you feeling more liberated since coming to The Bahamas?"

This comment brought laughter from both of them and it caught Laurel off guard because she did not realize she came on so forceful. On a more serious note, David shared how Ian said that their elections and change of governments were peaceful, which was good news for both of them. They were very familiar with elections in the African and some Caribbean countries which sometimes lead to violence; hence they were happy to know that regime change in The Bahamas was different. This however didn't mean there were no chances of problems occurring because Ian did state that the general strike of 1958, and the Mace being thrown out of the Parliament window by the late Sir

Linden Pindling, also former Prime Minister and the Hour Glass by the Late Milo Butler and former Governor General on Black Tuesday, April 1965 were instances when an uprising could have happened but the skilful leadership at the time was able to quell the crowd.

With their political history lesson behind them David shared with Laurel how the group continued to improve despite the fact that the election mode was in high gear. They have talked about Phillip's return and how each of them was expected to treat him. He told her that Ian had assured him that he felt the group would be supportive.

Putting those matters aside they both pondered over a letter they had received from Susan. Graduation from high school was due soon and she was looking forward to coming home to Eleuthera but she mentioned nothing about going to university. Was she going to surprise them and suggested that she return to the UK? Laurel was truly hoping that she did because some how she still believed in their educational system despite the fact that they wanted to live in this part of the world.

Chapter 34

*I*t was mid afternoon and Laurel was awakened from her mid day nap. David had gone with the young men to Harbour Island seeking jobs for them and so she wanted to know who would be at the door.

"Coming", she shouted from upstairs.

"Oh, Rachel come in. I was just resting. You look excited".

"Hi Laurel, Nina's son just returned home and he looks so good. I have already talked with him and I truly believed he has learnt a lesson from his past behaviour. You should see Nina she is smiling from ear to ear. I told her I would let you know the good news and I am sure David and Ian will lend her their support".

Rachel said all of this very quickly and Laurel was following her facial expression. Why would she come out of her way to tell me this information? Is there more to this than what meets the eye? She did not have to wait long for an answer.

"Laurel, what am I to do? I had a conversation with my neighbour and we have different views on politics and we just could not agree".

"Rachel, your political persuasion is your private concern and no one should influence that. Who you vote for is your personal business and it is best that you not share it especially if it is someone you know is of a different party".

"But Laurel what should I do we were good, good friends"?

Laurel wanted to give her the best advice and took her time formulating the next move. In the end, she felt that Rachel should approach her neighbour and talk about the incident that got them to the point where they were not communicating. Also, she encouraged her to discuss the issues that she felt needed attention in their community rather than idle talk. Laurel never missed an opportunity to assist individuals as well as enlighten them on things they should know about. With that information Rachel immediately began to identify the lack of employment for the young men especially and the fact that they needed more teachers in the schools. Laurel commended her for her foresight and looked forward to hearing that she had settled the conflict with her neighbour. Reflecting on the conversation, Laurel recognised that it was moments like that, which gave her satisfaction knowing that that she was able to give sound advice.

Shortly thereafter, David arrived home and was informed earlier in the day that Nina's son was home. Ian had already prepared a programme for the young man together with Mrs. Forbes the social worker and they felt confident that their help would be a great support to Nina and her family.

The rest of the afternoon found David and Laurel relaxing on their veranda, enjoying the sea breeze and making plans for Susan's return home. It dawn on them that they had not notice her mentioning George in the past letters or conversations. They knew she still was in contact with Janae but wondered what had happen to the friendship with George. Laurel who was not too keen on him was not too concern. This was especially the case when she reflected on the incident in Harbour Island when he influenced Susan and Janae to wander off to the Vic Hum Club. David on the other hand was counting the days for her to arrive and in a loud outburst he shouted two more weeks and Susan will be home.

In preparation for her arrival Laurel asked Sammy's Restaurant to make a guava duff and Sharil's for her favourite crack conch. David reminded her that she had to make a pitcher of lemonade. They were truly excited and waiting for her arrival.

All night there was a heavy rain fall and Laurel kept waking and wondering if the flight would be able to make it because from their experience rain delayed flights seem to be the norm. Looking lovingly at David she reflected on their early arrival to the island and on Susan returning after completing high school in the US.

Both Laurel and David got up to a bright sunny day. Laurel was extremely happy because later in the day they would be waiting at the Airport to welcome their beloved daughter home. She was hoping that Pineapple Air would be on time.

Pineapple Air delayed! That was not expected. Well, David understood from the agent that the rain they had during the night was now affecting Nassau but they assured him that the flight would arrive even if it gets dark because fortunate for the Rock Sound Airport they had lights for night flying. That was good news and so they both decided that they were not driving back to the Cape but would wait for the flight. This occasion gave Laurel an opportunity to meet up with old friends and even some of the students she had counselled at school.

At last, the plane was on the ground and appearing at the door was Susan and Janae, again there was no sign of George. What a reunion it was for both girls as their parents embraced them and all began to ask questions about their experience while waiting for the luggage. David even over heard Janae, telling her parents, that the College of The Bahamas (COB) would be her next stop. Is that the same for Susan? Is that why she has not disclosed her plans? What would Laurel say about that?

Driving home Laurel could not wait to hear what will be the next steps for finishing her education.

'Mum, I know you will not be happy but I want to be in The Bahamas and since COB has a teaching programme and it is my desire to teach here in The Bahamas'.

"Susan you want to teach said Laurel, your Dad and I thought you were interested in social work?"

"Mum, Dad that was a long time ago. I think I can make a meaningful contribution to The Bahamas by teaching the many young people in the community. One day I might even teach here in the Cape".

Laurel paused before she could respond and David looking out the window of the car, immediately noted that Susan had truly matured and no longer was the child that left home seemingly lacking self confidence. He could see that Laurel was struggling to answer but left it for her to deal with because he had no problem with Susan attending the COB, besides it would give them reasons to visit Nassau more often. He has heard from past students who did very well how they had to be focused and it would appear that the programmes offered were extremely good and from all accounts it was moving towards university status. Its development began in 1974 when they 'amalgamated the two Teacher's Colleges and the sixth form and evening institute of the old Government High School.

It gradually progressed in friendly co-operation with the University of the West Indies and several Universities in Florida, first offering a variety of diplomas and intermediate degree qualifications like an American Junior College and eventually to provide facilities for taking various external degrees'. He also remembered that the staff at Bahama House indicated that representatives of the college had been to the UK where they visited universities, all in an effort to strengthen their external links. This gave credibility to COB for attaining the much long awaited university status. Laurel never responded but this did not deter Susan from talking and bringing her parents up to date about what went on at her boarding school. Eventually she even mentioned how her relationship with George declined but she continued to be friends with Janae. It would appear that the quiet shy George began to move with a fast crowd once he left the island. This was not something that Susan was into hence the friendship which they had shared for so many years dissipated.

Once at home and having their meal Laurel revisited the issue of university and spoke about her disappointment. She wanted her to attend school in the UK but would accept her wishes and also commended her for the insight she gave for making the College of the Bahamas (COB) her choice and would support her in her endeavour. Both Laurel and David had brothers who were teachers and were pleased that she made that selection for her career. With that concern out of the way, the family truly enjoyed their meal and both parents sat beaming as they watched their daughter who previously gave them so much cause for concern but now seem to be a very confident young lady ready to take on the world.

Preparing for admission to COB was challenging especially waiting for information to come from her boarding school, nevertheless Susan and Janae both seemed to take it in stride while enjoying the summer holiday. Janae recently obtained her driver's licence and they were able to drive around the community and re-acquaint themselves with old friends. Additionally, Janae allowed Susan to accompany her to the Administrator's office where she was able to register to vote. While accomplishing such a feat Susan and Janae began to discuss the issues facing The Bahamas in general. Janae, feeling very grown up wanted to approach her first voting experience from a mature point of view rather than following blindly what her parents had expounded over the years. The exposure at boarding school gave her some insight into the community and how things could improve. She informed Susan that she had a number of questions she would like to address whenever the candidates visited her home. Susan was still waiting to be naturalised in The Bahamas, and therefore like her parents she was not able to register. However, she spoke with Janae about concerns and so together they compiled the questions that Janae would put to the respective candidates. Who knows, she may even be at Janae's home when the visit occurs.

While returning home from having lunch at Sharil's, they caught a glimpse of Phillip. Susan remark how thin he was but immediately attributed it to his problem and they both commented on his ability to overcome it. They were aware that her dad and Ian were lending support to his family and that the young male group were behind him, ensuring that he stays on the right path.

Arriving home after her morning drive in the community, Susan was surprised that COB had called to state that they had received all of her information and that she should come in for an interview to complete the process. Right away she called Janae, unfortunately she had not arrived home but she left a message with her mother. She hoped that the same information was passed on to her because they had been together so long; they both envisage being at the College together. Rather than waiting for her parents to come home she called each of them with the good news. She sensed the joy that her father displayed however, her mother was not very enthused. This bothered her to a certain extent, but she felt she was doing what best suited her. She strongly believed that being educated here in the Bahamas and obtaining her teaching practise here would put her in good stead to manage the children that will eventually be in her care. Sometimes she felt apprehensive especially when listening to tales teachers were experiencing in the class room, particularly in Nassau. Nevertheless, she intend to pursue her dream and feels she is up to the challenge. Would she still feel this way after spending the next four to five years at COB?

Chapter 35

A rriving in Nassau was exciting for Susan but Janae was not impressed, after all she was use to her space in Eleuthera where the traffic was almost non—existent. They both were season travellers so parents were left behind and they followed the instructions given by the Director for accommodations at COB.

"Ah Janae, is this the right place? This is where we suppose to stay?"

Janae was just as surprised as Susan. The place needed a coat of paint but she saw other young people scurrying about, taking in clothing and dishes, so she was certain this was their home for the next four years.

"Come on Susan, let's introduce ourselves, and find our rooms." Susan was closely observed by the other students although they were helpful in showing them where they were to take their things. The students in the room heard Susan's accent and asked her if she was from the UK. She said yes and no . . . I was born in the UK and moved to Eleuthera at the age of 12 and then to the US. I guess my accent is a mixture of all the places I lived. My name is Susan, what is yours? Janae also quickly shared with the students her relationship with Susan and that they had just arrived from Eleuthera. They had been friends ever since Susan's arrival in The Bahamas from the UK. That did the trick. They began to settle down and seemingly saw her as one of the crowd rather than focusing on her accent.

Susan was not phased by the noise and being her jovial self began to talk with those around her. From her efforts, she found that a large number of the students would be in the education programme and noted that the real reason behind this was to get a monthly stipend, which seemed to be the motivating force behind their reasoning for selecting that career. Well it was good for them but for her she would have to wait until her 'papers' were cleared.

Despite the outward appearance of the dorms, their room was okay and she was determined to make it work. Any complaining would only cause her mom to emphasise her wish for her to go to the UK. This experience she felt would even allow her to become more informed about the culture and really prepare her for the job she so wants to do.

With Janae by her side, already she felt that the students would be a friendly bunch to be around, she was looking forward to the orientation programme and the beginning of the college year.

David and Laurel once again found themselves alone, but this time knowing that she was only twenty minutes flying time from home. Their plans for a short vacation were already completed. They felt that the midterm break would be a good time to visit and spent some time with Susan before flying off to Stella Maris, Long Island. It has been on their agenda for awhile and with Susan being close to home they could now venture out and discover more of the Family Islands. They both felt that their voluntary efforts in the community were paying off and who knows, they may be able to take some of the young people to visit other Islands. That would be great and they could compare notes about different aspects of island life.

The End

Notes

Michael Craton, A-Z of the Bahamas Heritage,Macmillan
    Publishers 2007

Etienne Dupuch Jr, Bahamas Hand Book 1996

Isle of Wight, Internet Wikipedia

Cupid's Cay, Internet Wikipedia

Riots history, Sunday Express, August 28,2011, writer Graham
    Ball after interviewing Peter Ackroyd

Interview with High Commissioner Paul Farquharson, QPM

Carey Tanith, Where Has My Little girl gone, Oxford, Lion
    Hudson 2011

Preuschoff, Gisela, Raising girls, London, Harper Thorson

Gail Saunders, Bahamian Society After Emancipation, Kingston
    Ian Randle 1990

Experience Rottnest, Internet Wikipedia

Discover Fremantle and Western Australia, www.
westernaustralia.com

Singapore Tourism, Tripadvisor.co.uk

Harvey Roberts, Harbour Island, 1982

Wwwnc.cdc.gov/travel/destination/The-Bahamas.htm www.
lifescript.com

Anne Lionnet, Brillant Life Coach, Person Educational Ltd. 2nd
ed.2010

Rescue 'Lost Generation' The Times, United Kingdom
Newspaper, February 1st, 2012

The Islands of The Bahamas, The official UK website, www.
bahamas.co.uk

Michael Craton, Pindling The Life and times of the First Prime
Minister of The Bahamas, MacMillian 2002

College of The Bahamas website

Dr. Creflo A. Dollar, 8 Steps to Create the Life You Want,
Hachett Book Group, First Ed. 2009

Fr. John Culmer, Wikipedia

Canon Fr. Richard L. Marques-Barry www.
stagnesepisocalchurch/org/rector/fatherbarry

Canon Harry Ward, Comprehensive Family Ministries

Lightning Source UK Ltd.
Milton Keynes UK
UKOW01f1437141116
287622UK00002B/684/P